Danise C. DiStasi
and J. Ford Taylor

T·H·E
HIKE

The Missing Link to
Transformational Leadership

ISBN: 1439261431
ISBN-13: 9781439261439
Library of Congress Control Number: 2009910191

CONTENTS

"Effective leadership starts on the inside. If you don't know and accept yourself for who you are, how can you encourage and help others to be their best? Read *The Hike* and learn this important lesson of forgiveness and personal growth, and in the process, improve your relationships with everyone whose lives you touch."

- Ken Blanchard, coauthor of *The One Minute Manager®* and *Lead with LUV*

"Conveying a valuable, often abstract truth can be a very challenging endeavor. Such is the challenge Ford and Danise had in writing a book about relational leadership. However, by incorporating the principles in a story where we can all identify with many of the characters, we are able to grasp and apply the life-changing truths they teach in their Transformational Leadership seminars. This is a must book for anyone in leadership."

- Os Hillman, president, Marketplace Leaders; author, *The 9 to 5 Window* and *TGIF Today God Is First*

PROLOGUE

E very now and then a person comes into your life who challenges you beyond your own sense of ability; someone who gently prods you to think differently about situations, who sees your potential, even when you may not, and helps you to become a better person. And so it was with Dan's friend Ford.

"Ford, can you hear me?" Ford stared out the window with a faraway look, then sat up straight and drew in a deep breath.

"I'm sorry, Dan, what did you say?"

Dan laughed, turned a pen over and over in his hand, and looked at Ford. "I asked if you ever thought of starting your own company to share these leadership tools with others."

Ford nervously chuckled, looked out the window and blinked his eyes as if trying to revive himself.

Standing and stretching his long legs, Ford turned to Dan. "Why would others care or even want to know?"

Dan pointed to the whiteboard, every inch filled with names of current accounts. "Our company grew 50% because of the tools you've shared with us over the last several months. There must be something going on in your hippocampus that would make you think others might not be interested." They both smiled. Understanding the hippocampus was one of several tools related to how people respond to each other and how to build healthy teams. "Speaking of hippocampus, as transparent as you have been with me all this time, I know very little of who you were, only who you are now!"

"Well, who I am now is because of all the mistakes I've made along the way. All the tools I've shared are gleaned from what I have learned the hard way. I've only shared with you as a friend to help you and your team." He let out a slight laugh and shrugged his shoulders. "How on earth could I help others? There's no formal training, no program, no notes, no nothing!"

Dan's eyes closed as he laughed out loud. "Ha, really?" He held up a shabby notebook labeled "workbook" with papers sticking out everywhere. "But look at what your 'non-training program' has done! Lives have been transformed and families have been changed because of walking out what we've learned from you.

"In fact, I remember the time you casually asked me about my relationship with my father. I thought, 'why on earth would you ask that and what does my relationship with my dad have to do with my role as a President of a company today?'" Dan laughed heartily and ran his hands through his hair, shaking his head. "That was an uncomfortable place to go, but I learned later how much that sort of thing affects who we are, especially in business."

"Great observation, Dan," said Ford. "As you know by now, it has everything to do with how we operate in business. The problem is that we tend to mask what is so deep inside of us—whether it is in business or our personal lives, and we spend our time masking everything. By the time we are in the throes of our careers or family lives, quite honestly, we don't even know who we are anymore! And that's what I would call the great divide, which is the division between our real self and our ideal self or who we want to be.

"You see, as we grow up, so many things are spoken into our lives—countless words, phrases—some positive, and many negative. For me personally, the things that were spoken into me were that I need to be perfect and to be accepted. So I spent my life doing things to cover and mask my imperfections over and over and over again . . . just to be perceived as perfect so I'd be accepted."

Dan nodded his head as he listened to his friend open up, and then said softly, "That's powerful!"

Ford continued, "I truly believe when the light bulb comes on for folks in areas of their lives where they are wearing masks, one layer of the onion is peeled away, so to speak, for folks to be able to walk in freedom. My hope is that you and I walk out this transformation, others will want to know what is different about us and hopefully this process will free people from the burdens they carry. I'd love to be able to help people break through their constraints and really walk in freedom. Then and only then will people be all that they should and could be . . . individuals who take the time to do this to become better husbands, wives, team members, CEOs, better individuals all around."

"That's exactly who I want to be!" Dan took in a deep breath and looked at Ford. "Have I ever shared with you about one of the most powerful tools I've learned from the training?"

Ford shook his head slowly, "I don't believe so."

"It was affirmations! Man, the first time I ever gave my wife an affirmation—I will never forget the look on her face. I wish I could tell you that affirmation put a smile on her face. But instead, she looked at me with such disbelief. Why? Because I never spoke to her like that . . . ever. And I never realized it until I learned the importance of affirmations. My wife—the woman I love—had never heard an affirmation from me. Wow, what an eye opener that was. Oh, she heard an occasional 'great job honey,' or 'that's a nice dress,' or my favorite, 'hmmmm, this is a great meal!' But when I sat next to her, looked her in the eyes and said, 'Honey, tonight when I walked in the house in a horrible mood, it didn't affect you at all. In fact, you rose above my foul mood and complimented me, asked me questions about my day—you listened, you heard my heart and completely talked me out of my mood. In fact, you do that all the time and I just want you to know how much I love you for that.' That set the mood for the whole family dinner, which could have been disastrous, had I continued down the path I was on. Thank you for loving me enough to do that for our kids and me. That is just one of the reasons I love you so much.'

"She looked at me like she had a hard time believing me, like she was waiting for the other shoe to drop. Wow! Don't get me wrong, she knows I love her, but affirming her the way you taught us—look at the person you want to affirm and, use 'I–you' language, tell them what you liked about their life or something you may want to thank them for and be 100% sincere and genuine and not use the words, 'I want to thank you,' just go ahead and say thank you—that subtle way of stating the truth makes a huge difference in a person's life.

"But I was hit with a wall of distrust that I did not know was even there in my marriage until that very moment. I immediately recognized it and that moment opened the door for us to go to another level in our relation-ship—"

"Peeling back the layers," Ford said.

"Yeah, I'll say!" Dan sighed. "But let's get back to talking about how many more people can benefit from this training and how lives can be transformed."

Ford pursed his lips and looked straight ahead. "I appreciate the affir-mation, Dan, but I don't have any desire to run a company."

Eyebrows raised, Dan coughed, "What?"

Ford shook his head with a half smile, "Those days are over."

"Why? This could help a lot of people. The material on how to build healthy relationships is powerful, not to mention what we've learned about leadership, removing constraints. If more leaders could capture, understand and apply the very simple tools that are taught in this material, we'd be better leaders. In fact, I'd love to hear how the training came about for you and how you started this."

"You know, Dan, I'd love to tell you how this all came about. Do you remember what the two greatest leadership tools are when communicating a message?"

"Asking questions and sharing stories!"

"Yes, and I'd like to share a fascinating story, sort of a parable, of a guy who actually learned these very same tools and how his life was transformed after an interesting hike—in fact he would even tell you that he found the missing link to being a better dad, leader, coach, etc. His name is Stuart and he was a CEO of a very large company thanks to his contributions as a leader. He ran into some tough times, mainly because of his own poor choices, and hit rock bottom. He was fired and it was more than he could take so he started planning his suicide. . . ."

CHAPTER ONE:

The Suicidal C.E.O.

Stuart cupped his face in his hands and let out a low, painful guttural sound. "My God, how could this happen?" The room went dark and thoughts swirled as he slumped into a chair behind him. Nothing like this had ever happened to him before.

He pulled his cell phone from his pocket ready to speed dial # 5, just to hear her voice. The phone dropped as his hand trembled and he wiped the corner of his mouth. *Maybe I should call my wife instead.*

He shook his head to clear his thoughts. He retraced in his mind what had happened over the last several weeks to bring about this terrible news. Because of all the traveling involved in growing the company to $300 million, Stuart's life started to unravel, ever so slowly. He had asked the chairman of the board if he could step down as C.E.O. and take a position to support someone else in the role in order to continue and sustain the company's growth. He even recommended a gentleman who fit the role perfectly. The chairman agreed to meet and discuss such a proposition. After the amount of success the company had enjoyed under his leadership, it would be difficult to sustain the success without Stuart its leader.

Three weeks later, the chairman requested a meeting with Stuart and informed him that the board meeting had taken place without him. "The board decided to go ahead and hire your recommendation for the CEO position," said the chairman.

Stuart held his breath as he waited, knowing there was more to come.

"However, we will not need you to play a support role at this time. We appreciate your letting us know how you felt." The chairman reached in his coat pocket and pulled out an envelope. "We want you to know how much we appreciate all your hard work. We couldn't have done it without you." He handed Stuart the envelope.

After the realization of what was happening sunk in, the emotional devastation from those words left him speechless. His hands shook as he opened the envelope and tried to read the termination letter, but the words seemed jumbled and he couldn't make sense of anything. His mouth remained opened and words began to form, but nothing came out.

The chairman looked at his watch and said, "I've got to get going."

Stuart looked at him and whispered, "Can you help me at least understand why this decision was made so suddenly without us having a discussion?"

"It's probably best if you go home, take some time for yourself." The chairman walked out of the room and the door closed behind him, leaving Stuart alone, staring at the floor.

Stuart remained seated as he collected his thoughts. Once again, he picked up his phone from his lap, ready to hit speed dial # 5 and stopped. As though something snapped, his eyes widened and a plan began to take hold in his heart. He knew what he had to do. A plan he thought made sense, and he knew was best for his family. He nodded his head in agreement with his thoughts, and began to strategize the steps to take. His pulse raced as he tapped his foot. "Yep, this is exactly what I'll do," he said aloud.

As he stood to walk out of the room, he determined in his heart to see this plan through no matter what. *My wife and kids will be better off in the long run without me.*

CHAPTER TWO:

The Dark Voice

Stuart walked into his empty home, feeling the pang of loneliness, yet thankful he did not have to interact with any family members. Slowly placing his suit on the hanger, he carefully dressed in his casual clothes. He methodically placed one pill after another on the nightstand. There was no doubt in his mind that this was the best thing for his family. He was a failure and there was no need for them to be publicly humiliated by his actions.

As he continued to count each pill he carefully placed on the night stand, he thought of his life. He failed as a son, as a husband, as a father and now as a C.E.O. He stopped trying to figure out why he failed or how. He just knew the further he advanced in his career, the more he justified inappropriate behavior. The more powerful he became, the more others looked to him for wisdom and guidance. And the more accolades and praise he received, the more he needed. It became an insatiable hunger. He was unstoppable and could do no wrong, or so he thought.

He shook his head. . . . *32, 33, 34—that should do it.* He was taking enough anti-depressants to put down a horse. A few extra would put him out—for good.

Maybe I should leave a note. What would I say? I think my leaving will say everything. Besides, I'll leave the board's letter; she'll figure it out! Once she gets the money—that will help her get through this. Besides, once she learns what I've been doing all these years, she'll be glad I'm gone.

He sighed and looked at the framed picture of his family on the bookshelf. *Picture perfect!* His hand shook as he held the glass of water...pill number one, gulp, then two, then three.

He held pill number four in his hand as the pills began to take affect and numbness started to flow over Stuart like a warm wooly blanket on a frosty winter night. He settled into the feeling until a constant vibration slowly broke into his peacefulness. He opened his eyes, surprised to still be in his bed. He shook his head, torn between floating away and trying to figure out the interruption. Wanting to eliminate whatever stood in the way of him feeling the sensation of floating, he sat half way up and leaned on his elbow. The vibration of his cell phone brought him out of his stupor.

He grabbed the phone, pulled his arm back, and aimed for a place to throw it and glanced at the screen. Abe's number flashed brightly. He sighed and leaned his head back and closed his eyes.

CLICK. Just like that he was back to reality. "Hey, Abe."

"Stuart?"

"Yeah," he said in a clipped tone.

"Are you okay? Sound a little—um—you sound...are you okay?"

Stuart sat up, swung his legs over the side of the bed, looked over the pills on the nightstand, then at the clock, and rubbed his eyes. "Yep! What's up, man?"

"Just making sure we're set to leave tomorrow for the weekend."

"What's this weekend?"

"The hike? Remember? We talked about the date for this year's hike for a few months now? Stuart, are you sure you're okay?"

Stuart rolled his eyes, rubbed his forehead. "Oh yeah, yeah, Abe. Look, I'm sorry, something came up. I'm not going to be able to go this time. I'll pay for yours and mine and you go ahead and take someone else. I can't make it, I've got too much on my plate," he said as he continued to eye the pills.

"Stuart, you tell me this every year, and then every year at the end of the hike you come away refreshed and invigorated. So, you'll pick me up at 5:00 a.m. tomorrow, like we agreed. Okay, buddy?"

"Abe—really, I can't." His lip started to quiver as he took in a breath, not wanting to let his only good friend know what was going on.

His eyes suddenly widened. If this hiking trail were anything like the others, there would be plenty of dangerous twists and turns, cliffs and such. "Perfect!" he whispered as he envisioned himself accidentally tumbling down a rocky hillside.

"All right. I'll go."

"Atta boy, I knew you'd come around."

"You know, Abe, you're right. This is a perfect time for this hike," he said with renewed life. "We agreed I'd pick you up at 5 a.m. tomorrow, right?"

"You bet! Get a good night's sleep."

"Oh, I will," he smirked with a glint in his eye. He clicked the end button as he slowly moved off the bed and swiped the pills into his hand. With a dizzying step, he stopped to steady himself, and proceeded to walk into the bathroom to clean up.

"This could work out perfectly," he said to himself as he splashed water on his face. As his face emerged from the towel he used to wipe the water away, he scowled in the mirror and heard the familiar dark voice. *Just make sure you do it and don't make up any excuse to get out of it. Your family needs you to follow through on this.*

CHAPTER THREE:

Tell Me Something Good

Fog blanketed the cul-de-sac as Stuart turned into Abe's driveway. His long-time friend was already outside, his gear neatly lined up on the driveway. They exchanged warm hugs and, for a brief moment, Stuart wondered if he should share with his friend the desperation he was feeling. He pushed it all aside with the brush of his hand, as though removing a strand of hair from his eyes.

The shadow of the mountains stood in the background behind Abe's house like soldiers at attention. The foothills seemed to stretch toward them, beckoning the men to join their majesty.

Abe leaned back in the passenger seat and stretched his arm across the expanse of the two front seats. Stuart knew the sign. Abe wanted to talk.

"So, did you see the game yesterday?" Stuart jumped in quickly.

Abe shifted. "Yep, sure did."

"They better get it together soon or we'll be looking at next year.'"

Stuart squirmed a bit; knowing the clipped response from Abe meant he wasn't going to be sidetracked.

"So, how are you and Jill doing?"

Here we go. . . .

"Great, great, really well. How about you?"

"Good! Thanks! Hey, did you tell Jill and the kids this is a phone free zone?"

Stuart looked at Abe and then back to the road. "You mean there isn't any reception?"

"No, on this hike, they prefer you not use your cell. Some people don't pay any attention to that guideline, but trust me, you will enjoy yourself more."

Stuart nodded wondering if he could do without his phone but was willing to try. They drove in silence for a long time.

Abe finally turned to face Stuart as much as he could. "Stuart, I was a bit worried after we got off the phone yesterday. Are you sure you're okay?"

Stuart just stared at the long, winding road ahead, not sure if he should get ticked off at his friend or let everything out that has happened in his life over the last six months. He pursed his lips and swallowed. "Abe listen, I am just having a really hard time at work right now. Things are tough. I've not been myself lately, but that's to be expected sometimes, right?" He glanced toward Abe.

Abe nodded and looked toward his friend with a special understanding. Then he placed a firm hand on Stuart's shoulder. "No worries, my friend. I was just a bit concerned. I remember what depression sounds like and what I heard on the phone smacked me in the face with that memory. I would hate for you to be in that hell hole and for me to not reach out and help."

Stuart wiped his mouth, eyes darting back and forth. The word "depression" pricked his ears. Stuart thought back to the last few conversations with Abe, trying to remember if he had shared that he was on anti-depressants. He couldn't recall and looked at Abe with greater curiosity. *How could he know that? It doesn't matter. Everything is fine*, Stuart thought to himself.

Yes, said the dark voice inside, *that's right. All is well! Just remember you were only taking the pills because you are thinking of your family. This plan is best for them, remember?*

Abe looked at Stuart a bit longer, then turned and faced the front. Stuart sighed. It would be a long drive until they arrived at the foothills of the mountain they were to hike. The mountain was one of seven in this range and one that was unfamiliar to Stuart, but Abe knew it well. Abe had hiked this mountain many times with several of his coworkers, fellow board members and other executives. When he had described the mountain trail to Stuart some time ago, Abe laughed as he stated that he and others have blazed the trail for the younger ones coming up. In fact, they endearingly called it "Marketplace Mountain" because so many business relationships were developed while folks challenged the ominous trail. Apparently, according to Abe, many folks have been transformed by spending time on this hike. *Oh, I plan to be transformed, all right—into a dead person,* said Stuart as he silently laughed, thinking himself quite funny. The dark voice in his head laughed as well.

They finally arrived at a small, rustic cabin where a group of people crowded into a small room. Joshua and Grace, the licensed guides for the hike and his assistant, greeted them warmly. Stuart could have sworn there was something familiar about Joshua, with his engaging smile, deep voice, and piercing brown eyes. They grasped hands and shook firmly. Their eyes seemed to lock until Stuart felt vulnerable and uncomfortable.

Abe seemed to be very familiar with Joshua as brief introductions were made.

As Grace moved around to everyone, shaking their hands and engaging in small talk, Joshua clapped his hands together, rubbing the chill away and said loudly, "Soooo, let's get started. You all signed up for this hike understanding that this is our Transformational Leadership hike, correct?"

Everyone nodded.

"Good. Then let me ask you a question, you read the brochures or heard about this hike from a friend, right? I want to hear from you what your expectations are. Let's put it all out on the table. Tell me what you hope to get out of our time together"

Everyone stared at Joshua as an uncomfortable silence hushed even the soft awakening sounds of the early morning.

One gentleman spoke, "Other than fresh air and exercise and a beautiful view...we should have other expectations?"

"Sure hope so. You paid a lot of money for what you could do in your own back yard," said Joshua as he winked.

One woman said, "I understand this hike is similar to a ropes course in order to learn leadership. I hope I learn some fabulous techniques to be a better leader."

"Good, who else"

Stuart wanted to crawl into a dark hole somewhere and finish what he needed to do. The sooner he could get on the trail and find a place to kill himself the better.

There you go, you said it. See it's not so bad, right? And you're right, the sooner you do this the better off your family will be. Stuart sunk back into his chair and into the darkness.

"I am not only interested in learning new leadership strategies, I am looking forward to the first class meals I understand will be served on the hike. I researched several hikes and while I'm happy to rough it, I am a bit of a food snob and love the experience of gourmet food and fine wine, all of which will be served on this four day hike, correct?" said a young man barely above a whisper.

Joshua nodded and smiled so wide his large brown eyes became tiny slits under his brows. "You are absolutely correct. We'll definitely have some great meals together. What else?"

A very attractive woman raised her hand and remained silent until Joshua acknowledged her. Then she spoke. "From what I've read, it sounds like we'll learn how to have healthier relationships in order to be better leaders. Is that correct?" she asked coyly.

Joshua raised his thumb in the air and said, "Absolutely we'll do that!" Then he went silent for several minutes.

Stuart continued to look at the floor, embarrassed for the group that no one was speaking.

Finally, Joshua spoke. "Thank you everyone! We will achieve all the things you listed by the end of our time together. But, just be prepared. It will be different than your typical solemn hike or the latest and greatest leadership class. You know the kind where you sit in an auditorium and there is little interaction but they teach you all about leadership?? Or how many of you have been on a ropes course and things of that nature?" Joshua asked as he smiled and looked at each of the faces. "If you hang in there with me, I assure you, you will experience transformation. And best of all, we'll be doing life together. If you feel at the end of this hike that you did not receive your money's worth, we'll refund it. On the journey you will receive nuggets of wisdom. It will be as though you are on a treasure hunt. You'll also enjoy great meals and you will learn how to break down walls and build healthy, trusting, genuine relationships. Because without learning how to do that, we cannot be the leaders we want to be—nor can we have healthy teams, or families for that matter. Any questions?"

Everyone shook their head no.

"Okay then," Joshua said as he looked over at Grace. "Now, I'd like us to use these name tags," he said as his smile widened, listening to some of the groans as Grace passed out markers and name tags. "I know, I know. Every single group groans, but just go with me on this," he laughed heartily. Stuart actually felt himself smile as curiosity welled up within him about this fellow Joshua.

"Please write your first names on the tag, large enough for us older folks to be able to read." Joshua and Abe exchanged glances and smiled. Stuart felt a twinge of jealousy as he observed the interchange between the two men. He used to be closer to Abe, but in the recent past it was difficult to maintain the tightness of their friendship because of time constraints. Stuart stood up and tossed the marker onto an empty seat as he thought about Abe. Actually, time had nothing to do with it. He then heard a soft voice gently whisper a question. It was a familiar voice that he squelched every time he heard it. *Was it your own guilt and shame?* He cocked his head to the side wanting to hear the voice once more, but there was only silence.

"Since we're going to be together for some time, we're going to get to know each other really well before we even take a step toward those mountains. There are nine of us, and with some of the paths, twists and turns, we may need to depend on each other for our lives. Not unlike the twists and turns you encounter on your everyday hike through life. Now, everyone has a name tag, right?"

Everyone nodded as some took a seat and others stood.

"Excellent!" Joshua clapped his hands and smiled. "Before we get into introductions, somebody tell me something good!"

Everyone stared blankly at him. Joshua smiled wider.

Stuart turned his head to the side, rolled his eyes, and mumbled under his breath, "Great, any minute now we'll be singing Kumbaya."

Without looking at Stuart, Joshua said gently, "If at any time you feel so moved to lead the group singing such a song, Stuart, far be it from me to stop you." He gave Stuart a hearty slap on the back, causing Stuart to take a step forward. Stuart's face flushed from embarrassment.

"Come on, someone tell me something good!"

The chairs squeaked as people shifted and looked at each other. "Well," coughed a petite woman with fierce eyebrows and a name tag with bold print, 'Angela.' "This is my first vacation in five years—and I deserve this time off," she said as she moved her head side to side, emphasizing the words "time off."

Heads nodded and Joshua clapped. "Excellent!"

"Who else, come on—who has some more good news; work related, family, personal. Just give me some good news."

"This is my fifth time hiking this mountain," bellowed Abe. "I can honestly say each time I learn more and see more than I did before. So, I am looking forward to this hike and all the possibilities of what else I can learn."

"Yep, you're becoming an old pro, aren't you Abe?" Joshua smiled. "Come on, a couple more good things."

The next time you have a meeting or a family dinner, share something good with one another and see what happens!

More and more the group opened up and shared things about their families, the excitement about the hike, progress on work projects, etc. The interaction brought energy and lightheartedness to the group.

"Well," said a very attractive woman with the name tag 'Linda.' "I attended a women's retreat last month, and I loved it and am so very excited about this hike as well. In fact, I could hardly sleep last night."

Stuart rolled his eyes as her words dripped in sugary sweetness. Yet, he was caught off guard by the very disturbing, almost alluring manner in which she moved as she spoke. Joshua clapped his hands. "Wonderful," cheered Joshua!

Stuart lingered in his thoughts as he wondered about Linda and her story.

He would soon find out more than he cared to know.

CHAPTER FOUR:

Getting to Know You

"Okay, good job on sharing good things. As I said before, this hike is like a treasure hunt. You'll receive several different tools or treasures. It is up to you to decide if and when you will use the tools and how to use them properly."

Grace had a worn leather bag in her hand that looked like it had been on one too many hikes. She smiled as she reached in the bag. "Now you can't do much with "tools" if you don't have something to put the tools in, right?" She pulled a small leather bag out and threw it toward Abe who caught it effortlessly with his left hand. Grace threw another bag as everyone reached and laughed as if they were children at a Friday night football game waiting for a ball to be thrown their way.

Once everyone had a bag, they all looked it over. Some opened their bags, and others looked at Grace waiting for more instruction.

"Now you might've already noticed," she smiled with a crinkle of her nose as she leaned forward and whispered loudly. "It's empty!" She waited as others laughed. "But it won't be for long! This is your tool belt. Wrap it around your waist if you'd like and feel free to put an item into the bag if it is something you want to remember. Over the course of this hike, we'll be filling it up for you with various tools."

Stuart started to slowly warm up to Joshua and Grace. *Maybe these guys should be in corporate training rather than running around in the wilderness somewhere!* He chuckled to himself, "But then there's not much difference," he muttered.

"Okay, everyone," Joshua said, "we're going to get to know each other. I want to know who you are before I hit the trails with you and I want you to know me. Let's start building that foundation."

Joshua paused and looked eye to eye with each person as he scanned the room. Stuart looked away, not sure he wanted anyone to know him better.

"So, first I want you to come up with a positive adjective that describes who you are, your character. This adjective must begin with the first letter of your first name, such as Jovial Joshua."

Again, Joshua paused and looked around at each person and then asked, "Does everyone have a name?"

They nodded.

"Great, now we'll take turns and I want you to stand as you introduce yourselves. First give your name, adjective first then your first name and then answer these questions: Who am I? What do I do? And why am I here?

"Let's keep this to about two minutes each. I'll keep time and give you a signal when your two minutes are up. We don't have to go in any particular order. Whenever you feel like sharing, please just stand up and share. Okay?"

Angela crossed her legs and turned slightly away, pursing her lips. Angela moaned. "Remind me again what this has to do with hiking."

Joshua smiled a warm, loving smile. "More than you know, Angela, more than you know."

He then gave one short, sharp clap. "Now it helps to remember each other's names if after you introduce yourself, everyone says, 'Good morning," and then repeats the name. Alrighty, let's go," he said as he took his place to the side of the group.

Linda raised her hand, I'll go first. She moved around in her seat then raised her eyebrows, "Ready?" Joshua nodded as he looked at his watch.

"Okay, well, my name is Luscious Linda." She waited for everyone to repeat her name but they were still as they stared. "Okaaaayyy, well, I'm a mom of a beautiful 8 year old daughter who is going on 25." She laughed, "Not sure where she gets that." She looked down at her feet. "Um . . . I'm in sales and have been for years. Um, I'm pretty busy with that and my daughter." She looked down at the ground and said, "Oh. Why am I here? That's right, the third thing. I am here because I turn 40 next month and I've decided to do something really adventurous to prove I am NOT getting old. I don't have any pets, no time..." Her smooth, sultry voice

> *When you meet with a group for the first time, ask everyone to introduce themselves by answering the questions, "who you are, what you do, and why you're here!" How did it work?*
>
> *Think of a way to add your own twist to this introduction!*

carried throughout the room but Stuart wasn't listening. He was capti-vated by her lips until Joshua spoke as he gave the two-minute signal. "Time!"

"Oh, wow, already? Gosh I speak in front of people all the time. I'm not sure why this was so difficult."

Stuart continued to watch as she sat in the empty chair next to Angela. Angela crossed her legs in the opposite direction and turned the other way. He cleared his throat as he slowly stood. "I'll go if that's okay," he asked as he looked at Joshua. Joshua tapped his timer and looked at Stuart, "Go ahead, man!"

"Well, I'm Serious Stuart."

"Positive man, the adjectives are supposed to be positive," said Joshua.

Everyone said, with little enthusiasm, "Good morning, Serious Stuart!"

"I'm a Dad, husband—"

"Of a beautiful wife, I might add," Abe interjected.

"Yes, and two kids, a 7-year-old boy and," he smiled, "and a 4-year-old princess daughter who has daddy wrapped around her finger." He shuffled. "I'm a—a uh," he stammered, remembering he was nothing. He looked to the side hoping to hide his face. He took a deep breath. "I'm a leader, most of the time, a pretty good one, but there are times I am not so hot in the leader-ship department." He felt as though a dark cloud had come over his face. He rubbed his eyes. "In fact, the reason I'm here is because right now I feel like I'm a pretty lousy leader. Hoping I can rejuvenate my aspirations, redirect my vision, reconnect with uh—um reconnect with larger goals and," he looked up and smiled, "and nature of course."

As he looked up, for some strange reason he locked eyes with Joshua. He continued to speak but wasn't sure what he said. After what seemed an eternity, Joshua finally gave him the two-minute signal.

Stuart blew a sigh that almost whistled and went to sit down. He stretched his legs out, thinking, *I should have just said, I am a CEO. I tell people all the time, what's the big deal? They just let me go yesterday. It won't be final for another few days.*

Stuart rubbed his eyes and looked around. Then he sat straight up in the chair. He heard "Agreeable Abe" as he finished and then "Fretful Frank" was speaking as Stuart began to focus more. "Did he just say what I think he said?" he thought.

He's Linda's husband? How strange she never mentioned Frank being her husband in her two-minute speech. They don't seem to go together. Stuart shook his head as he thought to himself. *In fact, they seem total opposites.*

CHAPTER FIVE:

Are We Who We Say We Are?

Stuart leaned his head back and looked out the window. It was a beautiful day with the sun beaming through the trees. The leaves unfolded rich, fresh green colors as the season quickly moved into spring. The pansies stretched their colorful blooms toward the sun. The mountain was so inviting, it was difficult for Stuart to continue to sit inside. After all, he was on a hike for a reason—to be outside, to draw on the fresh air, to—*oh yeah, don't forget the real reason you're here!*

Angela stood up and put her hands in her pocket. "Well, I'm Angry Angela."

"Good morning, Angry Angela."

Joshua winced. "Angry?" he asked.

"Yeah," she responded as she moved side to side. "What's wrong with that name?"

"Are you kidding—angry?" asked Joshua as he shook his head side to side. "I said positive!"

"In my world," said Angela as she leaned forward and wagged her head, "anger is power and power is positive—or would Aggressive Angela be better." She looked up at the ceiling. "Nope, I'm sticking with Angry!"

Joshua shook his head and said, "Good morning, Angry Angela." Others feebly joined Joshua.

"I am happily divorced, no children, one cat. I am a systems analyst at a large company so I enjoy autonomy," she took a breath as she raised her brows and dug deeper in her pockets.

She looked up at the ceiling as she continued, "Um—oh, yeah. Why am I here?" She looked at Joshua, and squinted. "Do I have to talk for a full two minutes or is that the time you don't want us to exceed."

"Ahhh, a true systems analyst," he chuckled. "You have another question to answer."

"Darn," she snapped. "Okay, why I'm here. I just really need a break," her voice quivered. "I've been working hard, I really have no life and I just do not want to be around people."

Stuart leaned in to listen for the first time since his talk. He noticed Angela's face was no longer filled with anger but a soft sadness instead.

"I am really an introvert and," she slightly perked up, "if you don't know, being an introvert does not mean I am shy or backwards. It simply means that I get my energy from being alone. I love to write, hence the introvert part." Her eyes danced as she said the word write. "And while I need to learn leadership skills, I signed up for this hike because I was hoping to have some time alone. I need time outside and I love to eat. Mostly, I just need to reassess some things in my life," she said softly. "Like most people, I've had my share of disappointments, mostly from folks I've been close to. Part of me just thinks all people are crazy but then I have to wonder, maybe it's me! I hope I can figure that out while I'm on this hike—who knows."

Joshua applauded as Angela sighed and made a slight bow.

Doug jumped up and immediately started speaking. "Hi, I'm Doubting Doug and I am married, uh, well, actually separated. I hope not for long. I mean I hope I—we can work it out. No kids yet, love being outside. I'm sort of in between jobs. Um. I love to cook. I mean I really love to cook. I think I'm pretty good too. Well, I don't know, maybe I'm just an okay cook," he shrugged and shuffled his feet. "I'm here because a couple friends of mine came last year and I wasn't able to make it with them because I had knee surgery. They told me what a great time they had and how great the food was, so I signed up. It was especially life changing for one of my friends, so I decided it was well worth the bucks I had to put out." He glanced at Joshua, "Did I go over?"

Joshua nodded, "No, right on time, good job, man." He clapped as everyone joined in.

There was a long pause as everyone looked at Preston, then Grace and back to Joshua.

So they waited. And they waited. Preston waved his hand in the air and said, "I pass."

"You can't pass," said Angela. "You have to get up there just like everyone else. We have to hear your story too!"

Preston shrugged. "I don't think it's mandatory, Angela!"

Angela huffed and crossed her arms.

"Well what's your name, your adjective that is?"

Preston pouted his lip out and looked up toward the ceiling, "I think I'll go with Prideful Preston." He looked around as he nodded his head. "Yeah, Prideful Preston, that's good!"

"Guys," said Joshua, holding his hands like a 'T'. Honestly, I am so sorry if I've confused everyone. The adjectives are supposed to be positive, you know—uplifting, encouraging. I'm a little concerned about the names I've heard so far."

"What's wrong with these names?" asked Preston. "I take it from all I've read about this hike and what you've said so far, you want us to be real, and you want us to be honest, right? So, seems to me, if we feel like these names really describe who we believe ourselves to be, then we should go ahead and use them. I'm perfectly okay with it."

"Come on, geez," Angry Angela said. "We've come this far, can we just keep going?"

Joshua glanced at Grace who nodded her head and gave a slight shrug.

"You know," Joshua narrowed his eyes and tapped his finger to his chin. "You know, you might just be right. Your names are fine as is, so let's keep going."

Grace stood up and laughed a contagious, cheerful laugh. "Well, no worries, I am more than happy to jump in and talk, I have no problem doing that. I am Grateful Grace."

She stopped and waited,

"Good morning, Grateful Grace," said everyone in unison, with a tad more enthusiasm.

She touched the tips of her fingers together as she smiled. "I am the mama of Isabella, who is in college right now, totally enjoying herself. I love my life! What I do—I am an assistant to many of the guides out here in this beautiful mountain range part of the time, a business consultant part of the time and the wife of a wonderful, loving man who thinks I am the greatest ALL of the time." She laughed as did Joshua.

Stuart's eyes narrowed, wondering whether to laugh with Grace or be shamefully jealous that she exudes such joy.

Grace's face became suddenly solemn. "My life has not always been so wonderful and I will share more as we spend time together but," her eyes closed and in a second, her face beamed, "for now, I am thankful to be where I am on this journey called life. I'm looking forward to my time with you all! I will be with you most of the time, but on this hike I am really here to play the supportive role to my good friend Joshua, and now to all of you!"

Joshua applauded, "Thank you my friend. I am a blessed man to be able to call you friend. You have been such a treasure to work with! Thank you!"

"Thank YOU!" said Grace as she stood in the back of the room watching the group as Joshua moved to the front of the room.

Joshua rubbed his hands together. "The good news about going last is that if it is okay with you all, I'd like to take longer than the two minutes. Will that be okay?"

"As long as it's not two hours," said Angela. Most everyone smiled, which actually caused Angela to relax just a little.

"No worries, Angela," Joshua said softly as he reassured her. "My name is Jovial Joshua."

"Good morning, Jovial Joshua!"

"Good morning! I am Jason and Emma's daddy and Sherri's doting husband. As most guys will admit, I definitely married up." The men nodded in agreement. "What do I do? Well, I haven't always been a Ranger, guiding people on hikes. In fact, I have only been doing this for three years." He held his hands up, "Not to worry, I am exceptionally good at it because I have been hiking for over 25 years."

"I actually started my career in finance and worked my way up to an executive position. I was young and thought I was all that and more. I had a few pride issues, to say the least," he glanced at Preston, who was trying to sneak a peek at his cell phone and not looking at Joshua.

"I had this interesting thing going on in my head where on the outside I was big man in Corporate America, but inside I struggled with doubt, like I bit off more than I could chew and folks were going to find out who I really was. I was fearful that they would find out I wasn't really capable of doing the job I'd been given. I felt like a hamster on the wheel, you know," he motioned his hands in a circular pattern.

"I'll admit to having huge anger issues and then the more I experienced fear and doubt, the more I worked to get rid of it and prove myself, which continued to build up my pride—it was a vicious cycle. I'm pretty sure none of you have ever experienced this, right?" Joshua looked around.

No one moved except Stuart, who straightened in his chair and leaned forward.

"Well, anyway, I either had to be honest with folks and let them know I was struggling or I had to dig deeper and find a way to deal with it myself. Of course someone as full of pride as I was chose the latter, which led me to a life of 'socially acceptable drinking.'" He held his hands up and used his fingers to make quotes. "Yep, that helped drown out those thoughts of ineptness. But when you take a path such as I did, you need more and more of whatever it is that silences the voices so you don't have to face your fears." He shrugged his shoulders. Stuart couldn't help but wonder where Joshua was going with this, but his interest was piqued.

Did you recognize the different struggles each character displayed?

Do you struggle with any of the identified constraints?

"Pick your poison, folks: alcohol, drugs, affairs, pornography," Stuart's eyes darted back and forth. Joshua continued, "Working, eating, shopping, come on, we all have them. We all have a hidden place in our hearts where personal constraints hold us back from being the folks we were created to be. Our constraints hold us back personally, professionally and we never quite become the husband, father, friend, or CEO," he glanced at Stuart, "we were meant to be. We're actually stealing from the folks we love most and who we want to be near and with whom we want to be real in a deeper way. They are the ones we hold at a distance. We don't want them to see this gunk inside us. The people who matter the most to us in our lives are the ones who are short changed.

"What's this got to do with our hike? I am here because I got to a point in my life where my choices were a matter of life or death and I was pulled from the grips of death. Folks like Abe," he said as he smiled in Abe's direction, "stuck with me and made a difference in my life, and now I get to pass that gift on to other people."

Wow, so they do know each other. That's why Abe's so quiet. He's been on this journey before. That Abe—what a guy!

"I am here because I learn much more from people like you than I would if I donned a suit and sat behind a desk. There's nothing wrong with that; it's just not where I am supposed to be. So I hope to learn a lot from you all," he smiled, "but I hope you get much more out of our time together than some fresh air and exercise. I hope this is a life changer for you." Then he sat down, facing everyone, and the circle was complete.

CHAPTER SIX:

Affirmations

"Thanks everyone for giving us insight into who you are. Angela," Joshua said as he turned to look straight into her eyes. "Thank you for getting up to talk today." She looked at him briefly but then averted her eyes. "I know it was difficult. Thanks for sharing that you are on this hike to get away from people, and boy do I get that." He ran his hands through his hair and rested his arms on his thighs. "Thanks for sharing that you've been hurt by folks which resulted in disappointment; that is not easy to say. And whether you want to believe this or not, you have a great smile, and I think by the time this hike is over, we're going to put that "name" you gave yourself behind you."

Stuart watched the interaction between Joshua and Angela closely. Something very strange happened that Stuart tried to understand. *Did I see a chink in her armor? Did those words really get to her?*

Angela continued to look down but the minute she raised her chin, Stuart noticed her whole countenance had changed. Her eyes were bright and though she tried to suppress a smile, it peeked through.

"Thank you, Angela," said Joshua. He turned and was quiet for a moment, then softly said, "Based on what we heard folks say during their speeches, does anyone want to let others know what a great job they did?"

"I would like to say something," said Frank, sheepishly. "Thank you everyone. We've barely started and already I feel like I know you and would want to hike with you all. Usually it takes me a long time to open up and get to know folks. This has been great, so thank you."

Joshua clapped, "Good job!" Linda snapped a mirror closed as she smacked her lips to evenly distribute her lipstick.

Angela shifted in her chair. "Abe, you seem like such a quiet, gentle man. I was really impressed by the legacy you are leaving for your children and your children's children and how much you love them. You were always there for them and especially after your wife passed away. That must have been tough for you." Everyone was staring at Angela when she quickly said, "So thank you!" She stepped to the side with her head down.

I missed some of this in their speeches, thought Stuart. *Funny, Jill tells me all the time that I am never engaged, and I am always thinking of everything else.*

Abe leaned forward, "Well, I could not agree with you more, Joshua. In fact," he looked at Stuart. "Stuart, you are like a son to me." Stuart started blinking rapidly, *I'm not that much younger!* "Just seems like the Lord brought you into my life for a reason, don't know what it is yet, but maybe I'm not supposed to know this side of heaven. You make me think about things—things I have long forgotten. Lessons learned but tucked away and somehow we manage to get into discussions and I realize I have to pull those lessons out and dust them off." Abe's eyes moistened. "We've never talked about this, but you always make me feel like I have a purpose, like all the stuff I have been through was purely to share with you. Because the growth I have seen in you is amazing."

Stuart drew in a deep breath and held it. *My God, if he only knew!* Stuart wanted to burst into tears because he was living such a lie. He sniffed back the angst and fear and hoped no one noticed. "Stuart, if I am on this earth for one reason only," Abe, the big burly man choked back his tears, "it is to come along side you no matter what. Thank you."

Stuart just nodded and swallowed hard.

Doug clapped and said, "Wow, well said, man!" and Angela silently nodded as she blinked back what Stuart could have sworn were tears.

"Thanks, man," Stuart said hoarsely. He got up and gave Abe a hug, and the men smacked each other so hard on the back that it sounded like thunder, and the mood lightened.

As they sat down, Stuart's eyes darted back and forth and he swallowed hard. All the more reason he could not let anyone know how despicable a man he really was.

If you give genuine, real affirmations, you will see productivity increase, creativity flow, and bottom lines increase. If we focus on the relational part of our business before the bottom line or transactions, we'll see increased business. Marriages would improve as well if we practiced this.

"Good stuff, folks. Just think, if our workplaces were healthy cultures where leaders model and practice sincere affirmations, it would positively impact everything we do. Remember, the bottom line is transactional—affirmations are relational. Transactions are important, but they should not be our only focus. If you focus on healthy relationships, your transactions will be healthy."

"And the world would be a better place," smirked Preston.

Joshua smiled, "That's right, Preston!" If Joshua knew Preston was being sarcastic, he didn't act like it.

"Okay, let's get outside." Joshua headed out and barreled through the doorway, slamming the flimsy screen door.

Everyone followed Joshua and Grace and sat down on a few logs where Joshua directed them. Stuart thought it looked like a fire pit had been set up in the middle but the dirt had been smoothed over. Joshua grabbed a long, thick branch and drew a box in the middle of the pit.

"Somebody tell me what this is."

"A box," they all said in unison

"Good! What happens when we think 'outside' the box?" He put an x right outside the box.

"Good things happen!" said Doug.

"That's where ideas are formed," said Angela.

"Excellent," said Joshua. Then he drew an arrow to the inside of the box and he waited. "What happens if the ideas don't go well, you have an opportunity to do what?"

"Crawl back in the box," said Stuart, making an effort to participate.

Joshua pointed to Stuart and said, "Absolutely! We can always crawl back in the box. The purpose of this hike is to get you to think WAY BEYOND the box." Joshua drew way beyond the box and then scratched out the box all together. "In fact, we'd like to have you not even think of a box—the box is no longer in sight. We'd like you to think way beyond the bubbles."

"Bubbles?" everyone asked in unison

Joshua laughed. "I know it sounds crazy. Stay with me... Does anyone know why a bubble forms?"

Everyone shook their head no.

"I know—you think this is a trick question, right? Well, when the pressure on the outside is the same as the pressure on the inside, it forms a perfect sphere of liquid or gas—a bubble."

Everyone stared at Joshua. He threw his hands up in the air and shrugged his shoulders, "Crazy, uh? And when the pressure becomes too much, on the outside or inside—the bubble bursts and becomes smaller and more abundant bubbles. Wouldn't it be nice to be as flexible and pliable as bubbles? Continually stretching and moving? Well, you're going to be stretched on this hike. And while we exercise our legs, arms and quite possibly our hearts on this hike, we'll be exercising our brains as well. We're going to help you move from your box, to way beyond the box and move and stretch into bubbles!" Joshua looked around and held his hands up in the air. "Question for you...have you ever seen anything in nature created in a box shape?"

Everyone looked around at the beautiful surroundings and shook their heads no.

Joshua looked at the group and smiled. "The answer is no. Most shapes in our lovely created world are not in squares and boxes...they're pliable, flowing. And we're going to be thinking more in that mode rather than in boxes."

Think beyond the bubble!

"Okay, speaking of boxes," laughed Grace as she stood up. "Really, I'm not trying to confuse you— before you all head out, I have a small gift for you to put in your bag, the first of many tools, so to speak" She threw a small box to Stuart, then looked at the next small box and threw it to Angela, and did the same for the next box until everyone had a box. They looked at their gifts and opened them.

"Wow, this is interesting," said Doug as he held up one of several tiny candy hearts. "'Mine says, 'Doug, You Rock!'"

Angela laughed and said, "And mine says, 'Angela, you're awesome!'"

Everyone compared theirs with each other, for each one had a different inscription.

Doug packed his away in his tool belt and looked up at Grace. "That was pretty cool, personalizing candy hearts for us, but come on Grace. That's a tool? Give me a hammer or saw…candy hearts?"

Linda looked over her heart and smiled, "I kind of like it. It has my name on it, like the name tags we used and it's a heart. And who doesn't like hearts?"

"Yeah," said Angela, a little more serious. "I think the heart is to remind us to give affirmations, right?"

"Absolutely!" Grace and Joshua said in unison.

Joshua clapped his hands. "Now who wants to go on a hike?"

Everyone clapped and cheered, one person even whistled. The mood was definitely lighter than when the group first met.

CHAPTER SEVEN:

Social Anxiety

Al right, then," Joshua clapped his hands. "Let's get going. We'll head out of here and into the beautiful mountainous forest. You are all in for a treat!"

Linda zipped her bag and hoisted it over her shoulder. Frank tied his pack and dusted off a small smudge he found on the front. Joshua tied his boot strings, which lay comfortably over his dusty, well-worn hiking boots. He smiled as he watched everyone get their packs together.

The group continued to gather their material and prepare to move out on the hike, but they kept their eyes on Grace as she stood in front of the group.

"I won't be heading out with you at this time, but I will connect with you around lunch time. In fact, I will be at most of the dinners with you which is why I love my job! So have fun and I will see you all in a bit!"

As the team gathered their belongings, they all said their goodbyes to Grace.

"So, follow me, at least for a time," said Joshua. "Then we'll have some-one else move to the front for awhile…kinda' like a group of geese, but that's another lesson. Let's go." Joshua picked up a large polished stick that had writing on it but not in English. He held it and pounded it three times on the ground. The team finished gathering their gear, tightened their shoulder straps and one by one followed Joshua. It seemed as though the pounding of Joshua's stick was a signal to some unknown force; the team was together and heading in one direction,

Joshua walked with the stick moving in rhythm with him. The sun was warm and it was late morning already. They went around the building to pick up the trailhead. The trees shaded them from the noon sun, the moist green leaves cooling the trail immediately. Joshua led the way, with Angela behind him. Doug and Preston were next as they continued to talk. Linda took up behind them, and then Frank, who continued to fiddle with his pack, eyes darting back and forth checking out the trail as much as he could.

Stuart and Abe were the last ones. "So, Abe, what's the deal with this guy? Do you know him very well?"

"What do you want me to answer, what's up with this guy? Or how well do I know him?"

Stuart laughed, so typical of Abe.

"Actually, Stuart, I've known him for a long time. I only see him once in a great while, but we do know each other well. He's had a tough life for sure, and I hope you get to hear more of his story over the next few days. He's fascinating. Kind of reminds me of you!"

Stuart had just put a bottle of water up to his lips and took a sip, which he spewed out at the thought of him and Joshua being alike. "That's funny, Abe. We aren't alike at all!"

"Well, let's see what you think by the end of the hike."

Stuart watched the trail for a while and then looked up to see the expanse of the wooded area they were just entering. He caught his breath as the sun beamed through the tree line, illuminating particles of nature dancing and twirling through the air. He stopped and stared for a moment, then shook his head as he looked toward Joshua.

Stuart looked down at the ground again and started walking. His mind raced back to the mess of a life he was living. He had always been proud of how hard he worked and how far he climbed the corporate ladder. Every time he thought of how successful he was, he couldn't help but wonder if his dad would finally be proud of him. "Doubt it," he murmured to himself.

His dad was a hard working salesman—traveling salesman, they called them back then. He was always gone but he provided a decent home. God only knows what he was doing when he was on the road. But life was tough when he was home because of the drinking and physical abuse he inflicted on Stuart. Nothing he did was good enough for his dad. And he was punished for things he didn't do. Stuart hated him and as much as a young man could, he plotted to seriously hurt him several times over. Finally, he couldn't take it any longer. He ran away from home with $13.50 in his pocket, leaving a note for his mom.

Stuart managed to get by for a time until he tried to connect with his mom and his brother and sisters. He missed them so much. But when he called, he talked to his little sister and found out his mom had died. Stuart's eyes watered as he felt the pang of the words, "She died 'cause of you!" His sister spat into the phone as the angry words mixed with bitterness and sadness. "After you left, she cried all night, every night until she had a heart attack."

Stuart remembered hearing his father bellow angry words in the background as Stuart slid the receiver of the phone back into the holder. He vowed never to step foot in that town again—and he's never been back. He has not seen anyone in his family for over 25 years.

Stuart almost ran into Joshua who had stopped to take a swig from his water jug and wipe his brow. "How are you doing?" asked Joshua as he turned to look at the group.

Everyone else stopped as well and gulped their water as they nodded their head."

Joshua chuckled as he warmly looked over the group. He lowered his head and said, "Man, I remember the first time I went on a hike like this, I was scared to death. I had no idea what to expect. I had been hiking on small trails as a kid and into my teen years, but never the big hikes. My buddies, who were Eagle Scouts, talked me into it and of course I had to prove my manliness, so I went."

"So what were you afraid of?" asked Frank.

"Great question, Frank! You know how guys are, we have this little pride issue. In the boardroom I was fierce but outside of it—well my buddies were men's men. They knew how to fix anything, they knew how to survive in the wild, and they just knew stuff, I didn't."

Stuart spit his gum out and unwrapped a fresh piece. He had no idea how to fix anything. Not having a dad to watch fix things around the house, he paid folks to fix whatever he needed.

"To answer your question, Frank, I guess I had a fear of failing, perhaps? I didn't want to look like a fool, especially in front of my friends. Not only that I wanted to be successful on the hike. I was successful in everything else. I think all of us set out to succeed at what we do. And that first hike was no different."

Joshua continued, "Everyone experiences a bit of anxiety each time they do something new or meet with a new group or walk in to a new situation or place . . . *every single one of us*," he emphasized his words.

"But when the tour guide gave us name tags and walked through some activities similar to what we just did, what do you think happened to my social anxiety?" asked Joshua as he pounded his walking stick to signal it's time to walk.

"It was lowered?" asked Angela.

"You bet! So if we know people experience this, what are some things we can do to eliminate or at least reduce the level of social anxiety for folks?"

"Name tags," laughed Preston. "Can you imagine slapping a name tag on everyone every time they experience something new?"

"Actually, Preston, that is not too far off the mark. Imagine every time you have a new employee, what he or she must be feeling, or every time someone walks into your place of business. What if you wore name tags just to ease that feeling a bit for those folks?"

"Hmm," nodded a few heads. Preston shook his, "Yeah, like I'm going to do that," he muttered under his breath.

"One more thing, social anxiety increases when you are among peers! This morning, the majority of you probably felt some level of anxiety when you got up to speak, am I right?" Everyone nodded.

Social Anxiety is a combination of the fear of failure and the motivation to succeed. It increases when we're in front of our peers!

"Some of you were probably fearful of rejection or failure. When you sat down, how many of you really heard what the others had to say?" Everyone kept their heads down.

Joshua continued, "My guess is not many of us heard who was before or after us because we were so concerned with what people thought of our speech. Fear affects the behavior and the performance of one's team! So, what's the point of understanding we all experience social anxiety?" Joshua prodded.

Doug shrugged, "Man, I always doubt I can get to know folks in a crowd. Guess you are trying to loosen us up a bit? If I think about it and realize that everyone experiences social anxiety, it might help me to deal with it better, right?"

"Yep," said Joshua! "Whatever you can do to lessen social anxiety for yourself or others will lead to a more productive and fruitful time for you and your team—less time worrying about yourself, which is unproductive, and more time being focused on others. Just think about it. I won't even begin to tell you about the social anxiety I had the first time we ran into a black bear," Joshua let out a hearty laugh as he looked at everyone's faces.

Stuart was engrossed in his thoughts as he drifted behind the group a bit and watched Joshua and everyone as they laughed together. Fear was a normal state of mind for him. It gripped his heart with desperation and there wasn't a name tag in the universe large enough to mask his dark world.

CHAPTER EIGHT:

The Power of Forgiveness

After the group had been walking for awhile, Joshua led them to a small clearing. In the middle of the clearing was a beautifully hand carved wooden table with Grace leaning against it with a big smile.

"Hi everyone, I have box lunches for you, so help yourselves!"

The boxes were neatly stacked on the table. A big wooden tub located next to it with ice, a large jug of water on tap, and a tray full of fresh fruit bursting with vibrant colors. "So, let's grab a box and take a seat." Joshua went to the end of the table and sat down. He pulled out his netbook and started typing away while taking huge bites of his sandwich.

"Before we start into our lunches, I have a little gift for you." Grace pulled a handful of meshed netting out of her pocket and flung one to Abe, then another to Linda, Frank, Doug, Angela and finally Stuart.

"What are these?" asked Doug.

"These, my friends, are pieces of a net. Together they make a very strong net, not the kind that catches fish, but the kind that keeps you safe—a safety net. When you are afraid you may fall, or are fearful of failing or you're fearful to try something new, I want you to remember this net as a reminder of the tool we just gave you—everyone experiences social anxiety, which is fear of failure plus the motivation to succeed. Acknowledge that, be aware of that and do things to alleviate that for others as much as you can for yourself and others."

"And it increases when you are around peers, right?" asked Doug as he unzipped his tool belt to place the piece of net inside.

"That's right," said Grace as everyone moved on to eagerly open their lunches. A few examined the contents and nodded while others ripped open the paper casing around their sandwich. Stuart took a large bite and licked a dribble of mayonnaise from the side of his mouth.

"So how are we doing? Are you enjoying yourselves so far?" asked Grace.

Everyone had their mouth full of bread and turkey but managed a hearty nod and grunt.

"Hey, do you mind if we develop a tool together while we eat?" She waited and everyone shook their head in acknowledgement.

"Great, then let me ask a question…while we're together over the next four days, how do we want to treat each other?"

Everyone stopped chewing and looked at each other, then at Joshua, then at Grace. She repeated, "While we're together over the next few days, how do we want to treat each other?"

Finally Angela grumbled with a full mouth. "Hopefully with respect," she said as she pushed a piece of lettuce back into her mouth.

"Did you say with respect, Angela?"

She nodded emphatically.

"Great, keep going," said Grace as she was taking notes.

"Honesty," "With patience," "With kindness," "No back stabbing," The phrases were coming from everyone as each contributed based on how they wanted to be treated and Grace wrote them all down. Finally she stopped and held up the paper. "Let's see if I have this right. The question is how do we want to treat each other and ultimately how we want to be treated. With respect, dignity, kindness, honesty, patience—right?"

Everyone nodded. Abe, who was standing against the tree, said, "How about with love."

Joshua spoke as he folded his sandwich paper in a wad to throw in the waste basket. "There you go using the 'L' word again, Abe," smiled Joshua. "Grace, should they write that one in there?"

"Hold it," said Stuart. "Abe, you and I are good friends, and I can really appreciate where you are coming from on this. I truly believe you love everyone, like the good book tells us to. But honestly, that's stretching it a bit far for me. I don't even know these folks. Plus, when it comes to the people I work with, I think I need to keep 'love' out of it. I don't think you should mix 'love' and 'work'.'"

Abe pulled away from the tree and stood with his feet apart and hands in his pocket. "Yeah? And how's that working so far?"

"What do you mean?"

"How is not 'loving' the folks you work with working for you?"

Stuart lifted his shoulders and smirked, "Personally, I think it works great!"

"How do you think it would work if you did actually love the people you are around every single day, day in and day out?"

"I'd probably never get anything done," smirked Stuart as he looked around at the others to see if they were laughing.

"Then maybe it's not a matter of whether the word 'love' should be used, but whether or not we understand what the word actually means!" Abe leaned back into the tree and crossed his arms. "My sense is that we have no clue what 'love' really means, starting with ourselves."

Grace raised her eyebrows and looked around at the others and finally at Joshua. Everyone was silent.

"Soooooo," interrupted Grace, as she looked around at everyone. "Does the word love stay or go?"

No one responded. Finally Stuart held up his hand, "Go!" He looked at the others as if he dared them to go against his vote. Love was an empty word to him. Sure he loved Jill and the kids. But he's told other women he loved them too just to get what he wanted. *Abe is all wrong on this one, I know exactly what love means. It's a perfect form of control and manipulation.*

Angela looked away from Stuart and said, "The word love stays!" Preston said, "Definitely go," but Abe, Linda, Doug and Frank said stay.

"So we'll keep it." Grace continued writing. "Now there is something missing. What about not gossiping?"

"Oh, that's a good one," said Doug.

"Yeah," said Grace. "Gossip will kill a team, an organization, a family. So...no gossip; stay or go?"

"Stay," everyone said unanimously.

"Okay, one last thing . . . suppose we all agree on how we treat each other, what happens if one of us does not follow the behavior we agreed upon?"

"Call 'em out on it—big time!!" said Doug.

"Wait. I think I know where this is going," Frank said as he narrowed his eyes. "We should step back and make sure we understand what really happened, maybe something was just misunderstood. Then we should talk to that person one on one first before anything else, am I right?" Surprisingly animated, he grinned like a little boy who just won his first softball tournament.

"That's good, Frank!"

The team continued the painstaking process of working through each step of how to confront each other when an issue arises. Everyone participated and engaged in a lively conversation and shared many creative ideas. Finally Grace finished her writing and the team titled the document their "Covenant."

Grace put the pen and pad of paper down and placed her hands on her thighs. "You know, most folks don't like confrontation. In fact, we'll avoid it at all costs, but when issues bother us and we just brush them aside or bury them, they tend to manifest in other ways.

"The covenant process you were just involved in is one tool to help you deal with confrontation. Let me share a story that will give you another tool." Everyone moved in their seat, some stretched their legs but everyone leaned toward Grace. "I grew up in a really tough religious household. My family was 'super spiritual,'" she quoted in air. "I wanted nothing to do with religion so I was a little party girl. My very best friend's family was exactly the same way so she and I shared in the same rebellious streak. We weren't out right bad girls, just a little on the wild side.

"One night we were celebrating the end of our junior year in high school. We were excited about being the big, bad seniors so another friend of ours snuck a couple of bottles of wine out of her house and off we went to celebrate."

Stuart leaned in to listen to Grace. She seemed so serious and he was not sure where she was going with the story but her story struck a chord with him.

"So my friend, Suzy and I drove to meet our other friends whose parents weren't home at the time and we drank ...and we drank...and we drank.

"I felt fine and knew I could drive home and convinced everyone I was okay. After all, I only had a few glasses of wine, no big deal. And we were only a few blocks away, so Suzy and I got in the car, cranked up the music and sailed home.

"At least I thought I was fine. Suzy and I were singing and laughing, not a care in the world and in a second, my world went dark. I didn't see the red light and I didn't see the car that t-boned us on the passenger's side."

Everyone was perfectly quiet. Even the surrounding nature seemed to lean in to hear the heartbeat of the team as they held their breath.

Grace's lower lip quivered as her voice shook. "I was knocked unconscious and came to five days later in a hospital. I had no idea what happened. My mom was there holding my hand as I came to and she tried to piece it all together for me but none of it made sense to me. It still doesn't." She took in a deep breath.

> *Be intentional about establishing a covenant with your family and your team!*

"So imagine me laying in a hospital bed, badly messed up, broken leg, fractured skull. Fortunately that was all—hence the little limp when I walk, if you hadn't noticed. My mom tried to tell me all that had happened. She said, 'Gracie, you were in a bad accident. You and Suzy were drinking, you ran a red light and someone ran right into the side of your car. You were knocked unconscious and the impact was so bad that Suzy was pushed all the way over to your side of the car.'

"So I asked, 'how's Suzy, where is she? Is she here at the hospital too?' My mom just shook her head and cried," Grace whispered. "I never saw my mom cry like that. She cried so hard I couldn't understand what she was saying, and I was so upset. 'She didn't make it,' was all my mom could say. What the heck does that mean, she didn't make it? Mom," Grace's arms were flailing, her face twisted in pain as though she were right back in the hospital bed. "Tell me what that means?"

Everyone was still, some with their mouth opened, others leaned in further.

"'Honey, Suzy was killed instantly in the accident. Her funeral was yesterday.'" Grace wiped her tears that were now flowing down her smooth skin. Angela let out a high-pitched sob and Linda and Frank sat close to one another with their heads down. Doug sat with his hand to his mouth, staring and Joshua had closed his netbook as he and Abe sat quietly. Stuart turned away and swallowed hard, surprised by the rush of emotion.

"I killed my best friend." Silence. "I wasn't even at her funeral."

Grace spoke softly as she continued. "At the age of 16, I was charged with reckless homicide and served 23 months in a state juvenile corrections center. I was numb for twenty three months."

The six-step apology is:

1) *Acknowledge the offense*
2) *Say I was wrong*
3) *I'm sorry*
4) *Will you forgive me?*
5) *Will you hold me accountable not to do it again?*
6) *Is there anything else I should be aware of?*

Grace stood up and drew in a deep breath. "My family moved to get away from the criticism. They couldn't live with people judging them everywhere they went. They never saw Suzy's family after that. I finally got out of jail, completed my G.E.D. and then went on to college. I did okay but I was a walking zombie. Every day I was burdened with so much guilt and shame, I couldn't live with myself and I didn't even bother to mask it. I let everyone know how much I hated my life. But I didn't do anything about it. I just walked around like a zombie.

"Until one day I couldn't hold it in any longer. I got in my car and drove and drove and till I arrived at my destination. I pulled into the driveway of Suzy's old home, not knowing if her family still lived there and if they did, how they would react to me. I felt like my feet were made of clay as I walked up the sidewalk. I reached for the doorbell and suddenly the front door swung open," she made such a sudden motion it startled everyone. "And there stood Suzy's mom. She looked much older, and she stared at me for what seemed an eternity. I could barely look at her but when I finally locked eyes with her, I saw the warmth I remembered exuded from Suzy, and I broke down. She wrapped her arms around me," Grace paused and swallowed slowly. "She hugged me and we both wept together. She invited me in and we sat down not saying a word. Finally, I grabbed both her hands and asked if I could share something with her. I shared the details of the night Suzy was killed and what an awful mistake I made. Suzy's mom was quiet as she listened."

Grace brushed her hair out of her face and swiped a Kleenex under her nose. "I said I was horrified at what happened and not a day goes by, not a second that I don't think of Suzy. I wasn't trying to make her mom sad, so I tried to get through really quick. I said I was sorry and then I looked her right in the eyes and asked, 'Will you forgive me?' And I waited for an answer.

"It took her awhile, but I waited and finally she nodded, that was all she could do was nod and squeeze my hands. I told her how I had turned my life around and how I wanted to be held accountable to never do anything like that again. And though I have what we call our bumper people to keep me on track, I asked if she would help me stay on track. She actually smiled and even laughed and said she would be happy to do that.

"Then I asked one final question. Did I need to ask forgiveness for anything else? She hugged me and said, 'Yeah, there is. Why did you wait so long to come to me?'"

Grace let out a deep breath. "I didn't have an answer for her other than because I felt so guilty. We talked for hours and shared pictures and laughed and cried. I drove home that night and felt like I had lost 100 pounds. I felt so freed up it should have been against the law, but what a great feeling. Anyone care to guess why?"

Everyone moved as though startled by the question, but no one answered.

Grace held her hands out in front of her. "I asked for forgiveness…and received it. I am free. No longer imprisoned; not just by the jail time that I physically served for the consequences of my mistakes but by the jail time in my mind and heart. The good news is we can all be free from what holds us back."

Stuart narrowed his eyes as everyone slowly began to move around. He was so steeped in fear, anger, and lustful thoughts that forgiveness was no longer an option. And "freedom" was overrated. The only freedom he cared about was being in control, making money and doing what made him happy.

CHAPTER NINE:

What Does the Covenant Say?

Doug was the first person to approach Grace as she finished her story. He reached out to hug her. "Thank you so much for sharing. That must be a hard story to share."

"Thank you! Honestly, I can't even imagine what Suzy's family feels every time they share about Suzy," responded Grace as she held out her arms.

Joshua stepped up and reached for the covenant. "Thanks, Grace. I am always blown away when you share. Thanks for being so vulnerable and transparent."

"You're welcome, Joshua!" She lowered her eyes and her lashes brushed a tear away. "I know I am forgiven and I truly know why they call it Amazing Grace!" She slowly smiled as she said the words, radiating the joy in her life.

Joshua looked over the covenant. "So, during Grace's story, did you catch the treasure she gifted you with?"

"Definitely, don't drink and drive," said Linda solemnly.

"She made an effort to apologize!' said Preston with an air of arrogance.

"That was some effort, right" responded Joshua.

"Actually, she didn't make an effort, she did apologize and very well, I might add," said Doug.

"Indeed," nodded Joshua.

"She did a great job of apologizing," said Frank. "In fact, what I heard her do was acknowledge what happened. Since I mess up about 10,000 times a day, maybe the first step is to acknowledge I messed up and I was wrong!"

"Excellent Frank! What else?"

"You have to say you're sorry," said Angela.

"Good job," said Joshua as he leaned toward the group. "'You might even want to add I'm embarrassed by my actions. Next! What else!"

"She asked 'will you forgive me?'"

"Why is that important?"

"They have to respond?" asked Doug

"Yes, and once they do, ask them to watch your behavior and hold you accountable and give them permission to call you out on that behavior so you will never hurt them or anyone else with that behavior. What's next?"

"Uh?" asked everyone from the group

"What's next?"

Silence.

"What do you think it did for her relationship with Suzy's family when she asked that one simple question…is there anything else I need to ask forgiveness for?"

Everyone nodded as they looked reflectively at Grace and then Joshua.

"This is a tool and remember, this is the beginning of going from trans-actional—where we say 'I'm sorry,' to relational—'will you forgive me, hold me accountable, and is there anything else?'"

"Yikes," said Doug. "A little tough don't you think?"

"I'll let you all decide that during our time together," said Joshua as he signed the Covenant and handed the paper to Grace to sign and then had each one sign their names. "We'll have copies for you all tonight at dinner."

COVENANT

When we are together, we agree to treat each other:
With respect, dignity, kindness, honesty,
patience, love and zero tolerance for gossip!

If someone does not behave in the manner in which
we've agreed, we will:

1) GO TO THE PERSON ONE ON ONE: Assess the situation
and go to the person one on one.
The steps to take when you go to someone are
1) go in love,
2) in humility,
3) be ready to forgive, and with 100% of the truth.
We agreed to go to the other person with good intentions and
desire to understand them.

2) NEXT STEP: If the situation is not resolved, then we will
bring in a mutually agreed upon third party who will be a
witness to the words that are spoken.

3) NEXT STEP: If the situation is still not resolved, mutually
agree to bring in others (maybe three or more).

If no resolution takes place then some sort of separation

It is our intent that every issue will be
resolved by step one and no further action
will be needed.

Joshua looked at the group. "Ready to head out again?" He turned and looked at Grace who was picking up some of the bottles and papers. "Gracie, we'll see you later?"

"You bet," she winked.

Everyone formed a single line as Joshua moved at a pretty good clip. Stuart decided he should interact more so not to listen to the dark voice crowd in on his thoughts. His lingering thoughts ricocheted from being let go as CEO, to how he was raised to what is it about Linda that draws him to her? Stuart jogged to catch up with Preston. "Preston, I'm sorry, I didn't catch what you do for a living," he said as he caught his breath.

Preston turned to look at Stuart with his eyebrows arched. "I'm a turnaround specialist. I help companies like yours that have a self-proclaimed poor leader."

Stuart held his hands up, "Whoa! What the heck does that mean?"

"I heard your intro, and you said you were not a very good leader. Whatever your position is, if you sense you are not a good leader, I can only imagine what your company must be experiencing." Preston softened, "And I can help you with that."

"We've had enough outside consultants, thank you."

"Not surprised!"

Stuart looked around and realized that Joshua was way ahead, and there was a large break between him and Preston and the folks who were behind them. He yelled, "Hey, Joshua. Slow down buddy, some of the folks are falling behind."

Joshua stopped and turned. "Guys, can we pick it up a bit?" He winked at Stuart. Linda was noticeably lagging far behind. And behind her were Frank and then Abe.

Stuart kept walking but dropped behind Preston a bit. He couldn't help but wonder if Preston was really hurt by him not knowing what he did. Stuart remembered that Preston didn't want to share with everyone. *But he did hear my speech. Maybe he's just insecure . . . or maybe I really did insult him. Okay, enough of the self-talk babble.*

Stuart thought back on the covenant process they just finished. *We said if you are offended, you go to the person who offended you. Preston didn't exactly come to me one on one, so maybe I should just forget this. He expressed that he was bothered, and according to this covenant, I should go to him and acknowledge the offense. So quit talking about it already and just go do it!*

"Hey, Preston." Stuart caught up to him. Preston let out a sigh that Stuart ignored. "We signed an agreement—"

"Oh, that! A silly piece of paper! You don't think I intend to adhere to that do you?"

"Well, it seemed important to everyone else." Stuart straightened his back and appeared even taller, "Maybe we can try to live by it, I don't know. It's at least worth a try." An image of his wife flashed in his mind. How ironic that he hadn't kept the commitment he'd made to her. All part of climbing the ladder and having women come on to him, he always told himself. He shook his head to rid himself of the guilt that would not go away as it waltzed in and out with the dark voice. *Remember why you are here,* said the dark voice that he pushed down for awhile. *Remember it is because of all the things you've done that you need to follow through on your plan. At least make this commitment to your wife real. She will be better off without you.*

Preston looked at Stuart. "Hello, earth to Stuart."

"Yeah, okay," Stuart looked around nervously, as though others could hear the voice too. "Preston," he cleared his throat. "Clearly I've done something to offend you. If you explained what you did, I clearly missed it. I was probably thinking of other things, and I was wrong for doing that. I'm sorry—"

Preston looked directly at Stuart. "Stuart, quite honestly, I am just not comfortable with apologies. I'm not sure I've ever given a sincere one, and I'm pretty sure I've never received one. So this interaction," he moved his hand in a circle, "makes me very uncomfortable. But I do appreciate your efforts." He looked down at the ground. "It means a lot to me."

"Thanks, Preston." Not sure what to say, Stuart waited and walked. There were more steps to the apology that Joshua had explained earlier, he thought to himself, but he wasn't about to go any further.

> *Are you uncomfortable confronting others about an issue and sharing the truth?*

Sucking in a deep breath as though he could easily dispel that one last searing thought, Stuart finally spoke, and "So all is well?"

"Yeah, I'd say so," said Preston as he smiled slowly with a depth Stuart had not seen before.

They both looked behind them to see that Linda and the rest had fallen further behind again. Preston yelled out to Joshua, "Dude, slow down, these guys are really taking their time."

Joshua walked about 15 feet further and stopped at a small, cooler sitting at a fork in the road. In it were cold drinks, a fruit tray, vegetables, and trail mix. There were also brightly colored napkins, small plates, and cups. He pulled out a thermos and gulped down several swigs of water as he waited for the team to catch up, carefully observing each member as they gathered. From where Stuart stood he could hear snippets of Linda berating Frank all the way up to where the team stood in a circle.

"Well," said a winded Linda with a big smile as she wiped a gleaming bead of sweat from her forehead. "Nice of you all to wait for me."

Joshua took another gulp from his thermos, nodded and was noticeably silent.

CHAPTER TEN:

It's a Process

"So, how's everyone doing?" Joshua asked, wiping his mouth with the sleeve of his shirt.

Everyone nodded enthusiastically and gave a positive reply. Linda patted her forehead and asked, "How much further on this jaunt of the hike?"

Joshua laughed. "Linda, have you hiked before?"

"Sure," she smiled sweetly. "I walk all the time. I walk around my neighborhood, on the bike trail. I love hiking!"

Joshua smiled, shook his head and took another gulp of water. "Okay. We've gone half a mile and have three miles to go. How long it takes will depend on how well you keep up."

"Oh, I can keep up. So—I think while we're resting, perhaps we could talk a bit more about what this evening entails. I mean I know we're on a hike and all, but I paid a lot of money for a first class dinner and I want to know what to expect. Right everyone?" Linda turned to look at everyone.

Angela shrugged her shoulders as Frank looked down at the ground.

Joshua looked at her and said, "I guarantee tonight will be relaxing, refreshing and rewarding." They rested for a few moments not saying a

word but drinking in the surrounding beauty. Stuart was finding it difficult to engage with this group. The part of him that was the joker, the life
of the party, had the wind knocked out of him yesterday and the organized,
driven executive wasn't able to interact with this group.

Joshua tightened the lid on his thermos. His sudden handclap broke
into Stuart's thoughts, and he shook his head to clear his mind.

"Let's go. We have three more miles to get to our first night's stop. As
we're walking, let's stay together as much as possible. The path is wider
from here on out."

Joshua took his stick and pounded it on the ground as he forged ahead.
"So, let's walk."

Preston hopped over a couple of rocks to be next to Joshua and said, "I
must admit, I didn't think this whole covenant piece meant much, but Stuart and I had something happen and we at least started to use the covenant
and, I don't know," he shrugged, "it seemed to work. I mean, the process
seemed okay—better than I would have thought. At least we were talking
about an issue, right?" He looked at Stuart, who nodded.

"Yeah, we did at least talk, you're right! But, admittedly, it might work
great in this environment but not so sure about at home and really not sure
about a work environment."

"Okay, good, this is great discussion," said Joshua. "Can I ask a question? Why do you think we involved you in the process of creating the covenant? Why didn't I just hand you a piece of paper this morning and say,
'Here are the rules. This is what we have to adhere to while on this hike.'
Granted, we could have given you our safety rules, but how being involved
in understanding how we treat each other takes a team to another level."

"I doubt that we would have learned what we've learned so far had you
just given us a piece of paper and said do it," said Doug.

"Yet, that's what we do all the time, right?"

Everyone nodded. Frank said, "It's easier to craft an agreement of how
a group will behave or interact with each other and tell them rather than
go through the long process of what we did. People won't take the time,
everyone's in a hurry, especially leaders."

Joshua stepped over a small, easy-flowing stream and stopped before
anyone else could cross. He stuck his walking stick in the middle of the
stream. "Anyone know where this small trickle of water goes?"

Joshua pointed to their left and everyone's eyes followed the stream
until it dipped behind a rocky hill. "It heads due west and, little by little,

it molds the land it flows over, shaping it into a larger and larger body of water. It runs like this small stream for quite awhile and the reshaping is really unnoticeable until it is a larger body of water. Much like this small, seemingly insignificant stream, which really is the most important part of the ecosystem, is our entire covenant process today. Folks, there would be no large bodies of water if there were no small streams. There would be no large teams if there were no individuals to make up the teams. It is imperative each team member come together to go through the covenant process; yet most teams don't or won't put the time into the process.

"The *process* of what we've been doing is as important as the outcome, if not more so. The reason for doing it the way we did is so that you are involved in the process. He smiled and pointed to everyone, "And involving you will hopefully help you to remember, so that you'll understand *and* you'll want to excel."

"So, how significant is this stream?" Joshua pounded the stick.

"Well," Preston piped up, "though it contributes to a larger entity, until it becomes that entity, it really is somewhat insignificant. I mean, I get that this stream is important because it can become a larger piece, so its mission is to continue 'moving' toward its goal—to be part of a larger entity."

"Oh, really?" Joshua arched his eyebrows and then pointed to their right. In a small crook of the stream were three small starlings flapping their wings and splashing on their backs, chirping with a joyful melody. Then Joshua pointed to their left and there on a small rock with water running around both sides was a squirrel perched on its hind legs, its front claws close to its face, chewing rapidly. Then it dipped down close to the water and came up again. It sat straight up and looked at the group before it scurried off to an unseen, safe, secluded area.

"Insignificant? I would say their lives depend on this 'insignificant' stream."

Joshua pounded the walking stick and started walking. "It's all about the process guys," he said loudly. "This hike isn't about getting somewhere or you could get in your car and drive there. It's about the hike, the journey, and the surrounding beauty. This is not a one-time event. It is a process. Remember that! What appears to be insignificant isn't really at all. This stream is life to a squirrel and some birds and many other small critters. And the stream gave freely, having plenty of water to spare. Those of you who think you do not matter in the greater scheme of things . . ." he turned to the group. "You matter greatly to God!" They continued walking for some time.

"There's an old saying that has been retold in various ways over the years," Joshua continued walking and everyone stayed close, bending their ears toward him. "Let's see if you can finish a few statements for me in regard to what we've just been talking about and how we really learn and understand things. If you just tell me something, I am probably going to—what?—fill in the blank!"

"Forget," shouted Doug. "If you just stand there and preach something to me, I'm going to forget it. Like on Sundays, I *never* remember what our pastor talks about."

Everyone laughed and nodded.

"Exactly. There are some preachers out there with a great message, so why don't we remember what they say?"

"Because they are just talking *at* us?" asked Angela sheepishly.

"Exactly. If you just tell me something, I'm going to forget it. If I would have told you this morning, here's how we're going to behave, here are our rules, what then?"

"I doubt we would remember at all," said Abe. Everyone looked at Abe, who had been quiet for a while.

"Yep," said Joshua, keeping his eyes straight ahead. "So, tell me, I forget. Okay, now what if you taught me something, would I just forget that too?"

Preston said, "I might remember, that is, if it is something I am interested in or need to learn."

"Good," said Joshua, "so, 'tell me, I forget; teach me, I remember; involve me, I—what? —Fill in the blank!"

"Get it!" said two or three team members.

"Get what?"

"Get whatever it is you're saying. I get it, I understand it, I comprehend—" Angela said as she started laughing. "Dude, just tell me the words you want me to say and I'll answer it correctly," she laughed harder.

Joshua stopped. "Angela, if I tell you the answers you are likely to—what?

"Forget!" Everyone shouted together.

Joshua laughed and started walking. "You were right the first time, Angela. If you are involved in the learning or the process, you will remember. When my daughter was little, oh I don't know maybe two or so, I remember sitting down with her at her little table and getting the coloring book out and the crayons. Do you think I rattled off the directions to her? 'Here's how you do it . . . pick up a crayon, point it at the paper, see the lines? Now start moving the crayon back and forth on the paper and stay within the lines'."

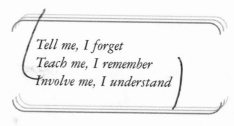

Tell me, I forget
Teach me, I remember
Involve me, I understand

"What do you do, Stuart, when you teach your kids how to color?"

"Uh," stammered Stuart as he tried to remember when he ever colored with his kids. "Guess the best way is to get down on their level, sit on the floor and just start coloring."

"YES! You color *with* them, and when they go outside the lines, you direct their tiny hands to stay within the lines and they can see what a difference that movement of their hands makes." Joshua was animated and spoke emphatically.

"You involve them!! And guess what—"

"They understand!" everyone said.

"Yes!" Joshua blew out a breath, pounded the stick and said, "And guess what folks?" He turned to face them and held out his arms wide, "We're here!"

Everyone looked just beyond Joshua, collectively took in a breath, and in one voice said, "Wow!"

CHAPTER ELEVEN:

What's a Hippocampus?

The shaded, winding rocky path they had been following opened into a beautiful soft meadow. The trees had parted their branches and were waving them toward the welcoming sunshine. Clusters of pink and yellow wildflowers dotted the meadow, and their fragrant aroma beckoned the group deeper into the grassy knoll. It was indeed a soothing sight for the weary hikers. In the middle of the meadow stood three cabins with stone paths leading up to them. Each cabin had its own unique style. The one in the middle looked more like a cottage; the two on the outside more rustic.

Stuart followed Joshua toward the meadow, enthralled by its beauty. Joshua pointed toward the cabins. "There's a road that drops down behind the cabins that our staff uses to get back and forth, but while you are on this hike, you will never see another human other than your team, nor will you see a car. All you will see are these majestic mountains and the most artistic display of beauty in creation itself," he said as he took in a deep breath. "Ah, I just never tire of this!" He laughed out loud, and the laughter echoed against the mountainside. Everyone else joined in, his laugh was so contagious.

He pointed toward the mountains. "There are hundreds of miles of hiking trails all around us—different terrains, various sceneries, all good. We'll be staying in these cabins each night but heading out from this place for daylong hikes over the next few days."

Joshua pointed upward, "Then, to top it off, we'll be heading to that peak right up there." Everyone looked up as they shielded their eyes from the glistening sun. "On our last night together we'll have a celebration up there. It will take your breath away, I promise!"

Hmmm, looks like a perfect place for an accident, spoke the dark voice in Stuart's mind.

"So, the rest of your gear is in the cabins." He pointed to the middle one. "Ladies, help yourselves to the chalet. Preston and Doug, head over to that one," he pointed to the one on the right. "Stuart and Frank, the last one's yours."

Stuart felt uncomfortable rooming with anyone, but especially with Frank. "Hey, if the married couple wants to be together, I'm cool with rooming with Preston and Doug. Maybe I'll just stay in Angela's room," he offered as he winked at Angela and smiled. Clearly he was hoping she would know he was kidding, but, just in case, he added, "Really, I'd be happy to stay with the other guys. Hey, what about you and Abe?"

"Tents, baby. No sissy cabins for me," laughed Abe.

"Seriously, you guys are sleeping outside? In tents?"

"Yep, that's what you do when you hike!"

"Okay, cool. I'm up for it. I'll sleep outside too."

Abe and Joshua looked at each other.

"What? You think I'm not man enough to sleep outside?"

Abe and Joshua chuckled. "Nah—we just don't have the gear, but we'll get it for the next few nights if that's what you want."

Linda yelled over the conversation, "Hey, do you all mind? Can I say something? I prefer that Frank and I have some time apart. We need that right now, right Frank?"

Frank was staring into the beautiful tree line opening where they had come from and muttered, "Whatever you say, dear."

"There, it's settled. Let's go, Angela," and she marched off. Angela followed, looking at the group, shrugging her shoulders.

"We'll meet for dinner at 6:30 p.m. on the patio, which is behind the cabins."

The duos headed toward their cabins to clean up a bit and rest before dinner. And, as promised, Abe and Joshua pitched tents. Stuart took a quick shower but left the cabin at 6:15 so as not to spend any more time than needed with Frank. As Stuart stepped out of the rear door of their cabin he was overwhelmed by the landscape. He walked down a naturally hardened set of clay steps and across a shallow stony brook path laced with petite white flowers. The flat grassy area was lined with huge oak trees that draped over the width of the area and touched in the middle, making a natural arch. Lights lined each branch of the trees, giving the area a soft, warm glow. Then Stuart noticed the long elegantly set table right in the middle. The sight reminded him of his honeymoon evenings in Tuscany, and he smiled. He closed his eyes and breathed deeply the smells of nature mixed with the wonderful aroma of deliciously prepared food.

"Beautiful, isn't it?"

Stuart's eyes flashed opened as he whipped around, startled by Grace. Because of her slight limp she seemed to skip into the area. "This is my very favorite spot," she said as she walked alongside where Stuart stood. "Reminds me of Tuscany!"

"Wow, I was just thinking that!" said a surprised Stuart.

"Hey, let's get some appetizers," shouted Joshua as he and Abe walked into the area. They greeted each other warmly. Joshua walked swiftly to the food table as he rubbed his hands together, ready to dig into his much-anticipated dinner. He lifted the lid off a chafing dish, while Abe headed for the cheese and fruit tray. As the steam rolled out of the pan, Joshua leaned down, closed his eyes, and took in a deep breath.

"Hmmmm, all this and heaven, too? Ha!" He reached his hand in, grabbed a flaky, cheese-filled croissant, and stuck it in his mouth. "I am hungry. Come on folks," he called toward the cabins, "let's go so we can eat!" Abe and Grace laughed and shook their heads.

Little by little the team drifted in, and stood admiring the view.

"Hey, before we get into our meal, I have a little something for you. This is to help you remember some of the things we learned today: Tell me, I forget. Teach me, I remember. Involve me, I understand." She reached in a plastic bag and pulled out birthday card size envelopes with names on it and distributed them to their specific owner. As everyone opened their cards, the area was filled with laughter and joy.

"Wow, when I opened my card, a recording of my introduction speech started playing—how funny!!" said Frank.

"Everyone has their speech recorded in your personal card." Grace looked caringly at Preston. "Preston, I am so sorry, but since you did not give a speech, you have an empty one right now. I'll show you how you can record something in it. You're going to want to do that before we leave and here's why."

She then looked at the others and said, "Keep this in your tool bag. By the end of this hike, I want you to write in the card your contact information and give it to someone and invite them to get to know you better. Everyone can only get one card. So think carefully about who you want to give this to."

"Cool idea!" said Doug.

"Can we eat now?" asked Joshua.

Grace swung around and laughed, "Yes, you may eat!"

Everyone filled their plate with food, took a bottle of water, and sat down at the table. Bottles of wine were on the table; the white being chilled and the red opened and "breathing."

Everyone was quiet at first as they savored their food. Doug poured a glass of red wine and offered to pour for others. Finally, Joshua spoke, "So, tell me something good!" Everyone broke out into a hearty laugh, remembering when they first heard those words.

Doug spoke, "Never in a million years would I have thought I'd have this much fun on a hike. I love hiking, but that's because I can be totally absorbed in my own little world as I walk. I can take in all the beauty and not have to interact with anyone. Every step of the way, I doubted that you knew what you were talking about," he said to Joshua, "or that I would want to get to know anyone here," he looked around. "My doubts have completely dissipated!"

"Really?" asked Joshua.

"Well, maybe not completely, but I'm working on it." To which he raised his glass. Preston did as well. "Here, here," they said in unison.

"By the way, at your place setting is a copy of the covenant you agreed to today." Some unrolled the parchment and looked over it as others put it into their tool bag.

Linda sat across from Stuart. She spoke in a sultry voice as she lifted her glass of wine, "I think this hike is a blast," she lowered her eyes a bit but kept them focused on Stuart, "I love the folks I've met."

Joshua gulped his food down and took a swig of his water. "Thanks, Linda, so, who else? Anyone else have something good?"

Abe shared that he had more energy than he's ever had in his life. Abe continued to share as others laughed and continued eating.

Doug raised his hand, "I have an affirmation." He swallowed and looked at Joshua, "Is it okay if we do affirmations"

Joshua smiled, "It is always okay to do affirmations."

"Great." He looked at Frank. "Frank, you seem like a really quiet guy—I bet we have a lot in common. Just talking to you while we were hiking earlier, it seems like you have a lot of wisdom. I am really impressed." Doug looked down and continued. "I just wanted you to know that."

Frank nodded his head. "Thanks, Doug. I appreciate that. I'm not really sure I deserve it but thank you!"

"Sounds like a hippocampus issue, Frank," said Joshua.

"A what?" asked the group.

"A hippocampus issue!" repeated Joshua. "Anyone ever hear of the hippocampus?"

"I know," said Doug. "It is a place where hippos go to learn."

Everyone burst into laughter. "You're pretty funny, Doug," laughed Joshua. "Wrong, but definitely funny! Anyone else have any ideas?"

Stuart tried to engage more and keep his focus on Joshua, "I think I might know. Or at least I have heard something about this," said Stuart. "The hippocampus is an area in the brain, right?"

Joshua nodded.

"It has something to do with memory, but I don't have a clue what or how it operates. Abe I remember you telling me about this," said Stuart as he turned to look at Abe who nodded in agreement.

Joshua cleared his throat, took the toothpick from his mouth and leaned back in his chair. "Well, Stuart, you're correct. It is a part of the brain. Understanding the hippocampus was a HUGE lesson for me. No doubt that it saved my marriage. It helped me learn to deal with so many people. It was my 'a-ha' moment.

"I shared earlier about pride issues and demons I was dealing with. One thing I struggled with was having numerous affairs and viewing porn—I am not proud of that part of my life at all. In fact for years, I hid behind a mask of guilt and shame. And just to make sure I buried that guilt good and deep, there was a little tiny piece of me that did things just to make my wife wonder if I truly had changed my life. I said I changed yet I always wanted her to wonder if I really did. That way if I fell again I could always blame her. Say that it was her fault because she never trusted me.

"Now that's crazy isn't it?"

Everyone nodded.

"But there was something in me that always believed I just never quite measured up and it was always someone else's fault. And it all goes back to that hippocampus. I had a need for attention so deep inside of me that it came out all sorts of ways.

"You know how as a kid, when you're doing something and you yell for your dad to watch?" he moves his arms up and down, back and forth. "Hey Dad, watch me, watch me?" His arms dropped to his side like a balloon that had deflated. "Well, sometimes they watch and sometimes they don't. But imagine your parents never watching, ever. That's me, my story. My parents were great parents, don't get me wrong. They just had too many kids and I was number nine. They were a little busy to notice what kid 7, 8, 9 and 10 were doing." Joshua laughed.

"We have great family reunions but nonetheless, in my hippocampus I wanted that attention and just did not get it no matter what I did."

"Then one day someone I worked with noticed me. She paid attention to everything I did. She thought I was smart and had all the answers when it came to knowing the business. She gave me the attention I always craved and then I needed it more and more. Because I never wanted to go back to that place of wanting attention and not getting it because that was an empty place for me. Here I had someone hanging around who loved giving me attention I thought I continually needed.

"There's a whole lot of medical jargon I can throw at you about the hippocampus. It is located inside the brain and is involved in memory." He took a long drink of water. "The hippocampus is associated with memories of events that we personally experienced and their associated emotions.

"Here's how it works. When an event takes place, your brain processes it and 'parks' it at the door of the hippocampus. In order to enter the hippocampus, it has to have two things associated with it. One, there has to be emotion associated with it. Two, there has to be a purpose associated with it, meaning something significant is associated with the event. If an event or very similar occurrences are repeated over and over, that information will be transferred to our long-term memory. So, the next time a *similar* event takes place, we don't go through the entire process of reliving that memory in the same way, we just start reacting. Over time, whenever anything that is closely related to a past experience occurs, we will have the same response automatically.

"The problem is this: many of our current responses to our current events are based on our earlier responses to totally unrelated events. Our responses, therefore, may not be 'accurate' given what is happening in the current situation. People respond to present situations out of their past experiences or pain. If I want to build healthy relationships, I need to be very aware of this fact and understand it. It takes a *new* learning experience to overcome the past learning—which can take place only with time and consistency."

Abe joined in, "So is that the self-talk thing going on in our heads?" Abe held up his hand as if he had a hand puppet on and it was talking in his ear as he asked Joshua.

"Yep, we say to ourselves, 'I've seen this before, I know what's going to happen.' And boom, before you know it, we're reacting as though we were way back in some previous circumstance, and we don't even know it. We treat someone we may be in a relationship with now as though he or she were someone from the past just because the 'emotion' feels the same. Do you know how many relationships are ruined because of this phenomenon?

"Let's say you had a stepdad growing up. He was a burly kind of guy, big booming voice, energetic, etc., and he beat you for whatever reason, say, not cleaning your room. Many years later, you walk into a cabin as you did this morning and see me, and right away you don't like me. In fact, you can't even look at me, and the more I talk, the more you do not like me. You're aware of this, but you don't understand your reaction. You're flat out nasty to me—why?"

"You remind me of my stepdad, who used to beat me. Not *my* stepdad, but the one in the example," said Doug.

"Exactly. You are going to react to me as though you would have when you were a child and feeling those very same emotions. But these are very real feelings, very real!"

"I get it," said Preston. "This is like déjà vu? Right?"

"You know we get asked that a lot," said Joshua. "This is not like déjà vu. The term *déjà vu* is French for 'already seen.' It is that strange

> **Hippocampus;**
> In order for a memory to move through the Hippocampus and into our long term memory (hippocampus) two things must be associated with the feeling:
> 1) Emotion or Passion
> 2) Purpose
> People respond to their present situations based on their past experiences or pain.

feeling you get when you think you've witnessed or experienced a *new situation* previously. When you experience déjà vu you almost always have a sense of eeriness or weirdness. Déjà vu is kind of like a dreamy feeling—whereas the hippocampus activity is very real based on very real experiences and emotions."

"So," said Angela, whose brow was furrowed as she seemed deep in thought, "Let's say I'm dating someone, a nice guy and he says something that triggers a deep down emotion in me and I react and get ticked at him."

"No," joked Preston. "You would never do that!"

Angela rolled her eyes and smirked. "Anyway . . . if I think about it, I'm not really ticked at him. It's what was said that took me back to a situation that had nothing to do with him, that could have been based on a reaction from something with my ex, right?"

"Right," nodded Joshua.

"No wonder I am always so angry, there's a lot of stuff back there. Who knew? So, how do we fix it? How do we get rid of that?"

"Well, good question! Do you really want to get rid of it?"

"YES!" said everyone emphatically.

"Now remember, there are also a lot of good memories in there! Do you want to get rid of them too?"

"No, just the bad."

"Okay, then *that* will take some change! And change is a process . . ."

"Not an event," laughed everyone together.

Grace stood up first and then lifted her hands, "Oh my gosh, I was so caught up in the hippocampus stuff, I almost forgot to give you your tool." She went to the dessert table and picked up a box. "Here you go!" She passed out a small key chain to each team member along.

Preston held it up and dangled the chain. "Is this for my Lamborghini?"

Everyone laughed.

He looked at it closer and said, "Uhl, this looks like a small Hippo." He peered closer, "It IS a hippo and it has the words, 'I'm free' on it. Umph, that's interesting...I'm free."

Everyone examined the key chain closer. Angela said, "It's missing keys."

"Very astute, you two! Perhaps you'll pick up a key here and there."

"Right," said Joshua as he stood. "And we've gone later tonight than we had planned. We'll talk much more about this over the course of the next few days! Let's meet here at 7:30 a.m. for breakfast, and then we'll head out. In the meantime, everyone get a really good night's sleep."

Everyone stood slowly, most not realizing how long they had been sitting there. Stuart was keenly aware of how long, because Linda had stared at him the whole time. He headed out first and went back to the cabin. Frank settled into bed quickly, but Stuart sat in the overstuffed chair in the "living room" section of the one-room cabin. He watched through the window as Abe and Joshua retired into their respective tents and listened as Frank snored loudly, occasionally shifting from side to side. Knowing he would not get any sleep, Stuart decided to stay in the chair and watch. No one knew he was afraid of the dark. "Must be a hippocampus thing," he muttered to himself and let out a small laugh.

He leaned back in the chair and rested his head. In a flash he jumped out of the chair and breathlessly looked around the dark room, then looked out the window. The moonbeams danced through the swaying fir trees, casting eerie shadows on the grassy knoll. Stuart narrowed his eyes and peered closer at the trees. His hands started to shake and then his whole body as he looked around the room again. He quietly sat back in the chair, "There's nothing here. There's nothing to be afraid of." But his body shook uncontrollably as fear overwhelmed him.

CHAPTER TWELVE:

The Pain of Change

Stuart leaped out of his chair when Frank barely touched him. "Geez, Stuart, you scared the life out of me. First I thought you were dead sitting in that chair and then you jump out of your skin."

"Where am I? What happened?" Stuart's arms were flailing as he tried to make sense of where he was.

"What are you talking about, man? Abe and Joshua were knocking on the doors bright and early. I'm surprised you didn't hear them. What are you doing in the chair anyway?"

Stuart rubbed his eyes, "Was I asleep?"

Frank swung his backpack over his shoulder. "You'll miss breakfast if you don't get going." The door slammed behind him.

Stuart rubbed his head and looked out the same window he had stared out the night before. He fell back into the chair as he started piecing things together. "What on earth am I afraid of? Am I that afraid of the dark?" he mumbled aloud.

Stuart tied his bootlaces, grabbed his pack, and ran out the door. Everyone was seated, their plates half empty. The billows of moisture from the steam table had simmered to a slow puff here and there. Stuart piled up eggs, sausage, and toast and started shoveling the food into his mouth.

"Stuart, slow down man. You're going to choke to death. We're not in that big of a hurry."

Stuart swallowed hard. He took a sip of coffee and swallowed his food. "Sorry, just really hungry." He wiped his mouth as he tried to avoid eye contact. He couldn't help but look in the direction where Linda was sitting. His eyes widened as he looked at her. She was laughing and sitting next to Frank. She had a baseball hat on and smiled at Stuart.

Grace was at the table and watched Stuart as he continued to eat rapidly. "So, Stuart, do you want to tell us something good?"

Stuart stopped with the fork midway to his mouth. "It's a new day man, that's all I've got to say!"

"You ready to hit the trail?" asked Joshua

"More ready than you will ever know!"

"Okay, let's pack 'em up and get moving." Joshua swung his leg over the back of the chair and started singing and snapping his fingers, "Move 'em on, head 'em up." Abe joined in and they belted out, *"Rawhide!"*

Everyone laughed except Stuart, who was inhaling his food and trying not to look at Linda. *You're not as strong as you think around Linda, are you? In fact, you're a weak little man when it comes to other women. You aren't fooling anyone. Just do what you came here to do,* hissed the dark voice.

Stuart rubbed his eyes. *Slow down Stuart. You don't have to figure everything out right now, just do the next thing.* With that, he took a deep breath and slowly exhaled. He picked up his pack, strapped it on and headed out with the rest of the group.

Everyone fell into line almost exactly as they had the day before except Abe was at the front of the line and Joshua was at the end. "Stuart, buddy," yelled Joshua.

Stuart didn't turn around but yelled back, "Yep?"

"You missed our time this morning when we shared all that we had done so far since we came together. So I'll ask you...what is the one thing you remember most from yesterday?"

"I have to say the info on the hippocampus. I remember Abe talking to me about that way back when, but I discounted it then. But realistically, I think I have a hippocampus moment every day, several times a day."

"Really," responded Joshua as he cocked his head to one side.

Stuart shrugged, "Yea, doesn't everyone? Not sure what you can you do about it though! I guess I could stop and think about why I react a certain way."

"Stuart, you are on the right track." Joshua stopped talking and pounded his walking stick as he looked ahead. Abe led the way, with Angela behind him, and then Doug and Preston. Once again there was a large gap before Linda and the people behind her—Frank, Stuart and Joshua. Joshua said, "Linda, I'm going to try to say this with as much love as I can."

She stopped, put her hands on her hips, turned and scowled at Joshua.

"We need you to keep up with the rest of the group. We're going to fall way behind if you don't."

Linda turned again and marched on. Frank shrugged his shoulders and followed Linda.

When Linda caught up to the others, Joshua said, "Okay, listen up folks, keep walking, but I have a question for you. Actually it's from Stuart. He said the hippocampus information was the most useful for him but wasn't sure what to do about it. He started down a good path with it . . . he said that when he experiences a hippocampus moment, he can stop and think about why he is reacting a certain way. So, I'm going to ask the group to help out with this. Like Abe said, this is a huge learning for all of us. In fact," Joshua pounded his stick as he stepped over a rock. "I would say this is one of the most transformational learnings I've ever experienced."

Doug turned his head to talk over his shoulder, continued walking and with a pensive look said, "I also think you have to stop, maybe that is the key, but how? Seems that once you are down that path of reacting in a certain way, it would be tough to just stop."

"Good and yes, I also agree. Once you are down that path, it is difficult, so it would take a total mindset change! How many of you like change?"

Preston and Linda emphatically raised their hands.

"Not very many people like change, right? Most people are uncomfortable with change. In fact, there's an old saying that goes something like this: 'People will seldom change until the pain of staying the same exceeds the pain of change." He stopped and had everyone gather around him. Joshua spoke softly. "You pretty much know my story, but here's the kicker and what it took for me to change. When we were first married, most folks would have called me a social drinker, a fun guy—a party animal, so to speak. But my wife wasn't laughing and my 'social' drinking got in the way of us communicating. As I continued to drink, there was a point where my wife actually packed and went to stay with her parents. We were married just a few months at that time.

"So I didn't suddenly come home to an empty house—my wife shared with me exactly what she was doing and why and what it would take for her to come back. I figured she wouldn't go through with it. And when she did and I watched her drive away—you bet I experienced pain. And as the days went on, that pain was unbearable. Within five days, I changed because the pain of staying the same far outweighed the pain of me making a change in my life. I still had a lot more things to change over time because of my stubbornness.

> *Change is a Process!*
> - *We take in information and process it.*
> - *Our feelings are stirred by this information, good or bad.*
> - *Our feelings influence how we behave, our actions.*
> - *Once we make a change and others experience it as well, only then can we make a difference as a team, family or organization.*
>
> *Are you experiencing change in an area of your life?*

"Change will happen—that's a guarantee. For most people, it takes some pain to move them off the dime. For some, they actively seek out change, and that's good. But most people won't budge until they hit a certain level of pain."

Joshua pounded the stick and started walking. Rather than maintaining the line, everyone kept pace in a loose circle around him. "Following the covenant like the one you've agreed to would be a huge change for most of you, yes?"

They nodded.

"Imagine doing that exercise with your family or involving your team to develop a covenant at work. Do you think that would be a huge change? As leaders," he stopped and looked around, "and yes, you are all leaders, and as leaders it will be necessary to walk the walk and be willing to move through change, difficult as it may be. *Remember,* this is not a one-time event; it is a process!!"

They continued walking through an open area of the woods. The sun was beating down on them as they made small talk amongst themselves. Joshua stopped at the next shaded place on the hike where a small table had been set with pitchers of iced water, baskets of perfectly ripened fruit and Panini sandwiches, freshly grilled.

Stuart laughed aloud when he looked over the table. "How on earth do you people do this? Just at the right time, just in the right place, just with the right food . . . and I never ever see anyone or even hear cars!"

Stuart turned around in circles, hoping to spot a mysterious employee.

"Stuart," Joshua put his hand on Stuart's shoulder. "They're here to serve you, not to be noticed by you. Now let's eat."

Everyone had already helped themselves. Stuart stood back with his hands opened and a skewed smile. *Why would anyone do that?*

> *Change!*
>
> *Change seldom occurs until the pain of staying the same exceeds the pain of change!*

Joshua shook his head, took a bite of his sandwich, and gulped down a swig of water. He nodded his head toward Doug. "Doug, tell us what you know about change."

Doug gulped, and then spoke. "Don't know much. Don't like it, never did, never will."

"Gee, Doug, tell us how you really feel!" said Preston. "I'm personally okay with change and I've had to really work through some tough spots in my life."

"Anything you want to share?" inquired Joshua.

Preston raised his eyebrows. "Well, I used to be a smoker. Everybody in the world knows that smoking is bad for you. You read about it, you hear about it over and over again. So in my head I know it, but deep down inside of me, I didn't want to change, I liked smoking. So I was really conflicted.

"Then my wife nagged me about it, but I ignored her for a bit. But when my kids started getting on me, the conflicted feelings began to gnaw at me. Finally, I had to change my behavior, I had to work at not smoking. As hard as it was I did it little by little. I thank God now that I don't smoke anymore which is one of the reasons I hike—so I can give myself a reward and a bit of motivation to never go back to smoking. And not only that, I was able to encourage my group of golfing buddies to stop smoking."

"That is a perfect example, Preston! We make this huge mistake of saying, 'if only my team would change, if only my husband would be nicer,' if only, if only—guess what?" Joshua leaned in as everyone else instinctively did so as well. "Nothing's going to change unless we change ourselves first—NOTHING! No Family, No Relationship, No Team, No Organization—Nothing!"

Everyone leaned back and nodded, looking at the ground.

"Ouch, right?"

No one responded. Joshua
pounded his stick and continued
walking. Slowly Doug followed, then
Preston, then Linda, Angela, Stuart,
Frank and Abe, single file. They
walked for a long time in silence, pondering Joshua's last remark.

Change is a Process!
No organization can get beyond the
constraints of its leadership,
processes or procedures.

Stuart felt some resistance. *I've changed drastically over the last few years.
I know I have. Why's this guy telling me I need to change when I can see all sorts of
flaws in everyone else? Why should I have to be the one to change?*

"What are you thinking?"

Stuart jumped, startled by Abe's words.

Stuart cleared his throat. "Nothing," he said, blinking his eyes rapidly.

Abe looked at him. Stuart shrugged, "I don't know, seems like I see a
lot of things in others that I just cannot be responsible for, things that need
to change in order for this 'collective unit' to work. And yet, I don't see
them making changes, but I'm supposed to change in order for things to
work between me and my wife or my family or my team or my board." He
looked at Abe, "Sorry, I just don't get that!"

"Can I ask you a question?" The others remained quiet, listening in on
Abe and Stuart's conversation.

Exasperated, Stuart turned to Abe, "Abe, you know you can."

"Stuart, what do you think you are really personally responsible for?"

"Other than the well being of my family, to make sure my company
survives in these crazy times," he gulped, knowing he pathetically failed
on both accounts.

"That's not it. It's even simpler than that."

"Really? Then I guess I don't know."

"You may have a ton of responsibilities, but you are only personally
responsible for just three things: your thoughts, your feelings, and your
actions."

"Ah, the three things about change, right?"

"Right!"

"So," Stuart continued. "Help me with this . . . I take in information in
some form, whether I read it, I hear something, or see something or I actually experience something, then that event generates a thought."

"Keep going."

"Okay, then from that thought, feelings stir up, right? Not sure I can control whatever feelings I get," Stuart scratched his head.

"Let's come back to that. Keep going."

"Then, based on those feelings, I behave a certain way, right?"

"Correct!"

"Then how on earth can I be responsible for my thoughts, feelings, and actions?"

"Why do you think we should *not* be responsible?"

"Hmm, good question! I guess I don't get how I can help my feelings? Which I guess takes me back to my thoughts." Stuart lowered his head as he recounted all the thoughts and voices and self-talk he heard all day long. No way is he responsible for that.

"Stuart, do you believe no one can cause you to behave or think in a certain way."

"Absolutely not! I don't agree. The guy who cuts me off in traffic, HIS actions are responsible for my behavior. The rude lady with the shopping cart that rams into my car . . . again, HER actions."

Personally Responsible for our:
Thoughts
Feelings
Actions

When an event occurs we can change the:
Thoughts
Feelings
Actions

Abe listened and then said, "There is a lot of material, Stuart, which supports that when an event occurs . . . *something* happens. The thought is generated, then a feeling is produced and then an action or reaction is chosen. Key word: chosen. That same research says, if the thought can be changed, the feeling changes, and then an action—most likely a different one—is chosen. I believe we are all responsible for all three of those. I'm not claiming that changing the thought is *easy*, mind you. However, *if* we can change the thought, *then* the rest happens; we can change our feelings and change our behavior. And if we take responsibility for changing our thoughts, we'll see a change in behavior."

Stuart jutted his chin out as he always did when he didn't agree with something and needed time to process. "I get what you're trying to say.

I just don't see how I can control what someone else does that makes me mad."

"Stuart, I didn't say you could control what anyone else says or does. What did I say?"

Stuart waved his hand, "Right, right, you said I am responsible for my thoughts, feelings, and actions."

Abe looked at Stuart, reading his friend. Stuart felt as though a dark cloud passed over his entire body as Abe lovingly patted Stuart on the back. "Let me see if I can help you. When my wife died, my son and daughter-in-law and their kids moved in with me for a while. They were transitioning from one home to another and I think they were worried about me." He smiled and winked.

"I remember I was slowly sinking into depression—I really missed my wife. I would have never told you that at the time, but looking back I was definitely depressed. So their timing was incredible.

"Well after living together for awhile, I started dealing with my sadness and coming out of that very sad time. And quite frankly, the additional roommates were wearing on me. I came home one night after a very long day and as I walked up the sidewalk I could hear the kids yelling and all sorts of noise going on inside. I walked in and my daughter-in-law was in the kitchen cooking and the kitchen was a mess and the dog was licking food off the floor, kids were yelling—you get the picture." Stuart nodded.

"Well, my first thought was, 'when are you guys moving,' or 'what a hassle' and that would have generated a feeling of resentment and I would have walked in, slammed down the mail, and my responses to anything they said would have been short.

"Instead, I immediately changed the thought. I walked in and said, 'hmmm, what smells so good?' Well, my grandkids were happy to see me, my daughter-in-law was excited to share what she was cooking for dinner, and my son was downstairs fixing a chair which needed work. I changed the thought, which immediately changed my feelings, which totally changed my behavior or actions.

"Imagine if I had gone with that very quick initial thought of 'what a hassle?'" I would have ruined everyone's mood that evening—and we would have all been miserable. And my changing the thought, then changing the feeling, then changing the actions eventually led me to move out of the sadness I had over losing my wife."

Abe continued. "I still feel that I am responsible for my thoughts, no one else. I take that responsibility. I encourage you to give this a try on something and see how it goes. Think of something that causes you anger or sadness, and try to change the thought around it. See if the feeling changes; I believe it will. Again, I am not saying it is an easy process, especially around issues like death, or abuse or many issues, but it's worth a try on the little ones. And just like Preston's story about not smoking— try changing the thought, changing the feeling, changing the behavior or action a little at a time; one step at a time. One of my favorite sayings is 'Be transformed by the renewing of your mind.' The process of renewing begins with you being personally responsible for changing your thoughts, then changing your feelings, changing your actions."

Abe leaned down to pick something up off the ground. He looked at the bronze coin, flipped it over a couple of times in his hand and then reached in his pocket for his knife and worked on scratching something on the coin. Finally, he flipped it toward Stuart.

"What's this?" asked Stuart as he opened his right hand.

"Just something to remind you of our talk on TFA!"

Stuart looked over the mud laden coin with the scratched letters TFA. He clenched his fist around the coin and looked longingly at the sky with a pang in his gut. *Would my life have been different if I had done this one thing— change the thought, change the feeling, and change the action?*

CHAPTER THIRTEEN:

How We Communicate

Linda sped up to be closer to Angela. "So Angela, I know you said you were 'happily divorced' but do you or did you ever want children?"

Angela's face twisted as she shrugged her shoulders. "Not really." She did not turn to look at Linda as she spoke.

Linda nodded and then whispered, "Do you notice anything weird about Joshua?"

Angela then turned to Linda, her brows arched, "What? No! Is that what you want to talk about? Joshua?"

Linda used her hands to try to quiet Angela. "No, no, not at all. I just think there is something funny about him, don't you?"

"Like what?"

"Like is he for real? Do you think he's very genuine? I mean come on, he acts like he has his whole life together but I doubt that. He's a man right? Do you know any of them that have their act together?"

Angela paused as she looked straight ahead at Joshua and continued walking side by side with Linda. "I think Joshua's on the up and up."

"You do? I mean, don't you think he's a bit controlling? He acts like we're a bunch of school kids."

"We're on a hike, Linda and we paid him to be our guide. And I am not very comfortable talking about this any longer."

Linda smiled and leaned in closer to Angela. "Well, just watch him more closely and you'll see what I'm talking about." She kept her smile as she looked straight ahead.

Joshua turned around and looked over the group. Linda and Angela had fallen far behind. He took out his thermos, chugged down some water, and patiently waited until everyone caught up. "How are you doing?" he asked.

Linda took out a towel and wiped her face, smudging what little makeup she had on. "I'd like to make a suggestion of how we can make this hike more interesting." The towel muffled her voice as she wiped over her lips.

"Let's do an exercise to get to know one another a bit better." She looked around enthusiastically, wide eyed and smiling.

Doug opened his arms and asked, "As if we don't know each other well enough? Why would you want to stop in the middle of our hike to get to know each other?" He shook his head as he shrugged his shoulders.

"Who said we had to stop?" She said with an edge to her voice. "Let's keep moving, and I'll explain what I think we should do."

"Linda, why do you think you have to control everything?" asked Angela in a quiet voice as she slowly sat down on a large boulder. Joshua stood and watched the interaction, saying nothing.

Linda snapped her head around to look at Angela. "You know, Angela, I get that a lot, especially from women who are just jealous of me. Just because I am a natural-born leader, you people want to label me some kind of control freak." She sneered as she continued to walk toward Angela slowly. As she got closer, she softened her voice and leaned down over Angela. "Well I have news for you . . ."

"Whoa, whoa, whoa," said Angela. "Linda, what is your problem?"

"You asked me a question in front of everyone. I answered the question in front of everyone." She batted her eyes and held her hand over her chest. "Did I do something wrong?"

Angela leaned back as her eyes widened. "Well, you got all up in my face wagging your head and finger at me, with this nasty tone of voice..."

Linda cut her off, "Frankly, Angela, I'm not sure why you are making a big deal out of this. I was answering your question. It is no big deal to me, what is *your* problem?" and with an exasperated sigh, she emphatically rolled her eyes.

"Well, you're proving my point of you needing to be in control!" Angela waved her arms as though she were pushing away an unwelcome visitor.

> **How we communicate:**
> *55% Body Language*
> *38 % Tone of Voice*
> *7% Actual Words*
>
> ** Albert Mehrabian*

"Were do you get off calling me a control freak?"

"I didn't call her a control freak," said Angela as she opened her arms and looked at the others as though she were looking for support. Everyone looked in every which direction so not to lock eyes with Angela.

"Yes you did, Angela. You said exactly that," spewed Linda.

"I don't think she actually used the words 'control freak,'" chimed in Doug, "but she inferred it."

Joshua stepped into the middle of the group. "Okay, now hold on folks. Let's not read more into this than what actually occurred."

Linda sweetly smiled and lowered her eyes. "I was simply making a suggestion for us to make this hike more interesting and Angela just goes off on me."

Stuart looked at her, dropped his jaw and then looked at Joshua. Joshua kept his eyes on Linda.

"Linda, I am not so sure about that. What I witnessed in your body language and tone of voice demonstrated a very different message."

"I know what I heard, Joshua," snapped Linda. "She called me a control freak, now can we just move on?" As she jerked her back pack, the contents fell out. Linda scurried to pick up the contents as Joshua leaned down to pick up her mirror. He reached out to hand it to her. She hesitated to take the mirror from Joshua but then reached out as she looked up into Joshua's face. Stuart was surprised by Linda's expression which looked like she loathed Joshua, but then quickly lowered her eyes.

"Usually the first thing we do when we hear something that strikes a chord in us is to immediately react and assume the worst."

"No doubt," said Angela. "There must be something in me that cannot stand women who need to be in control."

Joshua looked at Linda as though he were waiting for her to have an a-ha moment. She shrugged and looked away.

"Good observation, Angela. Remember the hippocampus? We all bring our own hippocampus stuff into our communication with others as well, and it almost always slams up against the other person's hippocampus stuff." He slammed his fists together in illustration. "I imagine Linda had a hippocampus moment as well.

"Being really careful how we communicate, especially when something upsets us is really important for our relationships. Do you all agree?"

Everyone nodded and said, "Yes!"

"I remember so many times, I'd be sitting there with my wife stewing about something, anything—maybe something she said or something that happened that had nothing to do with her. And out of the blue, or so I thought, she'd ask me, 'Are you mad at me?' 'No!' I'd snap at her. 'What makes you think I'm mad? I'm not mad at anyone!'"

"She would just get up and go in the other room. Needless to say, we were not communicating very well. That is, until I realized how much my body language revealed what was going on inside of me. Again, another lesson I've learned the hard way, but it sure helped me start communicating better."

"Let's keep moving, shall we?" he said as he continued to look at Linda. She tightened her pack's straps and started walking.

Joshua pounded his walking stick and took the lead, walking ahead of everyone.

Doug spoke as he quickly stepped out on the path. "We humans, men and women, sure seem to have a horrible time communicating. We take cheap shots at each other with words, hide behind e-mails and voice mails—if we could ever learn to read body language. Well, I doubt that would make any difference in my ability to communicate, but it sure makes sense to me."

"How many of you have heard, 'sticks and stones may break my bones, but words will never hurt me!'" Joshua asked. Everyone raised their hands.

"Who thinks that's a lie?"

Everyone but Abe put their hand down.

"Words only make up 7% of the message, but they can cut right down to the bone," Joshua sliced the air and made a whoosh sound. "They hurt, no doubt words can hurt."

Preston said, "Makes you think about the e-mails where all the letters are capitalized?"

"I have to believe that the person who sent it is mad at me?" Frank asked sheepishly. You can tell by the *tone*," he lifted his brow, "in which they were said—the capitalized words . . . that's a sign that the person's being forceful."

"Or they just forgot to take the 'cap lock' off?"

"Yeah, most of the time just by the words . . . you can tell they're ticked," said Preston, slowly nodding his head.

"So do words hurt?"

"You bet," said Doug, and the others nodded.

Preston narrowed his eyes. "Hmm, this is an interesting discussion, Joshua." He pointed a finger up in the air, "I had something happen just recently. I'm on the board of a nonprofit. One of the lawyers we work with found a record that said we owed money to a lawyer the group previously worked with. So he emailed the lawyer explaining this and confirmed we would be sending the check. And signed it, 'Thank you.'

"The response he received from that lawyer was, 'No thank you.'

"He printed the email and showed me and asked, 'What do you think of this? Sounds like he doesn't want it. I'm not sure what to think.' I laughed when I saw the response. So I grabbed the paper, I put a comma after the word *no* and underlined the word you so that it read 'No, thank you! Send the man the check.'"

Everyone laughed and nodded. "Great story, Preston," said Joshua.

Stuart thought back on the last conversation he had with his wife, Jill. He had to think back a ways, but in the depth of his mind, most of the conversations over the last 10 years were almost the same. He would engage on the surface, but his heart was elsewhere all the time. Sometimes it was on an issue at work, or a difficult conversation he had with someone, or another woman, but it was never where it should have been. By the time he got home, he was always so spent emotionally and physically, he had no energy for anything else in his life. *I wonder what my body language or tone of voice was demonstrating.* It was easy for him to put the thought out of his mind because it was almost too much to think about. Now that was something he was really good at—bury any thought that would take introspection.

CHAPTER FOURTEEN:

Digging Deeper on Subtle Truths

Stuart walked alongside Joshua. "So Joshua, why do you do this leader-ship stuff on a hike? Wouldn't you make more money if you did this in a corporate setting?"

Joshua pounded his stick as he threw back his head and bellowed a laugh. "Actually if I got paid every time someone asked me that question, I would be a rich man!"

"I have to tell you, I am not an introspective guy, but some of the things you've been sharing have really made me think. I'm serious about you doing this in companies. But then again, I guess the points you are making have a lot to do with being on a hike or journey, so to speak."

"You hit the nail on the head, Stuart."

Stuart continued, surprised by his sudden desire to engage. "I have to admit, I was not very impressed with you when we first met. I mean, you seemed like a nice guy, someone I could have a beer with but your story and your transparency—well I've changed my mind about you."

Joshua stopped and everyone else stopped as well. "So Stuart, are you telling me I made a bad first impression?"

"Well, I'm not sure I would say it was a bad impression. I just wasn't very impressed. I mean, don't take it to heart."

"No worries, but I want to make sure I set it straight. So what was your first impression of me?"

Stuart cocked his head and shrugged his shoulders. "Well," he stretched his neck. "I thought you were sort of a, well, a," Stuart stammered trying to find the right words. "I don't know, just some redneck—if it is politically correct to use that term?"

"Well then, I'm really sorry I made that type of impression…"

"It's not your fault, Joshua! Maybe I…"

"Let me finish if that's okay?"

"Sure—sorry!"

"Will you forgive me?'"

"Of course, I'm not sure it is necessary to ask…"

"And will you hold me accountable to work on making a good 1st impression with others?"

"Well, I'm not exactly sure how I could do that because I probably won't see you after this hike!"

"Is there anything else you'd like to share that I may have done since we've been together?"

Finally Stuart dropped his arms to his sides and asked, "Why are you saying all this? Shouldn't I be the one apologizing if I had the wrong first impression?"

"Wait a minute," said Doug as he stepped over a log and moved closer to Stuart and Joshua. "I know what you're doing. You just walked out the apology that Grace laid out yesterday, right?

"You're a genius, Doug! I am hoping that we're beginning to understand going from transactional—where we say 'I'm sorry,' to relational—'will you forgive me, hold me accountable, and is there anything else?'

"That's good," said Stuart. "I've coached some of our interns as they were graduating from college and looking for jobs on how important that first impression is. It can take you a lifetime to undo a bad first impression, and most of the time—you don't get another chance."

"Exactly right, Stuart!" Joshua stepped forward, somewhat energized as he pounded his stick and walked as the others walked faster to follow closely behind. "A first impression is sometimes referred to as a "moment of truth" because people believe that what they are seeing or hearing or perhaps even feeling is reality—that is, the truth of the situation. No matter that their first impression is merely a mental picture of less than one moment in time. Yet people think of it as real." Joshua turned to make sure everyone was keeping up. The team almost tripped over him because they had been walking so close.

A first impression is made in 30 seconds or less.

It takes 20 additional good encounters, or one sincere apology, to undue a bad first impression.

It takes milliseconds for our brain to decide to enter a website.

Angela spoke up. "Maybe if we know we've made a bad first impression—key word *know*—then we should apologize for it."

"What do you think that will do for your relationship with that person?"

Doug looked up, "It would make a world of difference. But not everyone can so easily apologize to people, Joshua, like you do."

"Good point, Doug." Joshua said, as he lowered his voice. "Think about this," said Joshua as he pounded his stick with each step. "We all have a hippocampus with all sorts of stuff, we all experience social anxiety, and we all make bad first impressions. All this stuff," he swirled his hands in a circular motion, "comes into play when we meet folks and then we try to build relationships and working teams.

"What if we fully understood all this in our core being, and we took the steps to get past these constraints. What if we were committed to building real, honest, and genuine relationships? Do you think our divorce rate would drop? Do you think our friendships would be more lasting and less draining? Do you think our organizations might be incredibly effective, not to mention profitable?"

"Sign me up," said Stuart. *Leadership gurus have said this stuff for years—and failed! What makes Joshua so different? I can't put my finger on it, but he is different!*

Joshua slid his hand into his pocket and pulled out an envelope. He handed everyone a gift card.

"Ohhh, I love The Coffee Shop," squealed Linda as she looked at the gift card. She looked up with a smile and a gleam in her eye, "Let me guess. This is for us to build real, true relationships, right? You want us to take someone to The Coffee Shop and build a relationship. Great idea!!"

"It's a tool. The ability to build relationships that are real and true will provide the foundations for strong families, healthy and productive teams and a better you! When you take someone to have coffee, use the tools you've learned so far, and see what happens. Be intentional!"

Stuart looked at the gift card. *Jill loves The Coffee Shop. I wonder if she would be open to having coffee with me sometime!*

Stuart walked quietly as he thought about what Joshua had said. He shook his head, clearing his mind. *I have to admit . . . this stuff does make sense. I never realized how much garbage we bring into our relationships.* He lowered his head as he thought of the relationships he'd destroyed and how he was on the verge of ruining his marriage.

"I've got to get free of this," he muttered to himself.

"What did you say, Stuart?" He didn't realize Linda was walking next to him. She reached out to touch his arm and he quickly pulled back.

"I'm sorry, I thought I heard you say something."

He shook his head no. But as he looked up at her, his eyes lingered longer than he meant to, yet he couldn't turn away. He finally broke away from her stare and stopped walking. He leaned over his boot and pretended to tie his laces as Linda continued walking.

Then Joshua said, "Let's step it up so we make it back in time to relax a bit before dinner. Linda, how about you lead the way . . . we'll follow you on today's last leg of the hike."

Linda's eyes widened, "I have no idea where I'm going! How am I supposed to lead?"

"Just follow the trail, Linda."

"But—but the trail goes in a bunch of directions," she stammered. Everyone continued walking but slowed and waited for Linda to take the helm.

Joshua repeated, "Just follow the trail."

Preston stopped and put his hands on his hips, "What? Why on earth would you do that? Talk about slowing down throughput by having the slowest member lead the team!"

"Spoken like a true consultant," laughed Joshua. "Can you break that down for us a bit, Preston?"

Preston raised his eyebrows and leaned forward, saying slowly, "Why would you choose the slowest member of the team to lead us on the rest of our hike today? You're slowing us down, so we can't possibly get to our destination in the allotted time. That makes no sense to me what so ever. Help me with this."

Linda waited.

"Linda, go ahead and walk."

She huffed as she turned and started walking.

"Preston, I'm going to ask you to watch this for awhile and then I want to see if you can figure out the method to my madness."

"Not going to work," said Preston, shifting his backpack.

"This is scary," muttered Frank as he looked down at the ground.

"Let's just walk, everyone," smiled Joshua, pounding his stick as a sign to move forward.

Linda started, Joshua followed, and then Frank, who continued with his head down. The team stayed close together, but they maintained an eerie quietness as they walked through the low-hanging tree branches. All you could hear was the occasional squawk of a hawk flying over and the crisp sound of twigs breaking underfoot. The sun seemed to barricade itself behind soft, billowy clouds. Beyond the picture-perfect playful clouds were dark ominous ones that looked ready to burst with a deluge of rain.

Stuart lowered his head and scowled. A struggle ensued in his mind and heart. A part of him wanted to hear the dark voice, it was all consuming but at this point in his life, a very comfortable place. But somewhere in the broken clouds appeared a ray of sun that pierced through the darkness with a voice that said, *all is not lost*. Stuart wiped his brow, not wanting to believe there could be any hope.

They walked for almost an hour and a half in silence, Joshua speaking only to point out various trees, plants, flowers, and creatures. They walked single file and at the same pace, and no one lagged behind.

"How are you doing?"

Everyone nodded and said, "Good."

"Any questions about anything so far?"

"Yeah, I have a question," said Doug as he jogged to be next to Joshua. "What is the tie-in between the hippocampus and your whole change theory, you know, change the thought, change the action."

"In one sentence, can you tell me what you believe the hippocampus is all about?"

Doug closed his eyes, but then opened them quickly so not to trip over any stones. "It's the part of your brain that allows the thoughts and feelings of an event to enter into your long-term memory." He scrunched his face and peered out of one eye at Joshua. "Can I do it in two?"

Joshua laughed, "Absolutely!"

"If an event happens enough times and has emotion or passion as well as purpose it goes through our hippocampus and is stored in long-term memory, and we react to *current similar* events based on the thoughts and feelings we had before, which sometimes causes us to behave like we behaved before." He pointed a finger in the air. "Even if the original event happened way back when we were children." Doug beamed at Joshua.

"Good job! Excellent, in fact," Joshua laughed heartily. "Now, we all agree that we are personally responsible for our thoughts, our feelings, and our actions or behaviors, correct?"

"Yep, you got it!"

"This may be simple, but it certainly is not easy. Intellectually, we understand this, but walking it out is another story."

"This may be simple, but it certainly is not easy. Intellectually, we understand this, but walking it out is another story.

"There are times you cannot help the first thought—guys looking at a woman on a beach or women receiving feedback from a man and feeling like they have been rejected. But once you know this information you will be much more aware of your feelings. At that point you can step back, pause, and ask yourself, 'Where is this coming from?' Many times you will immediately relate it to a *similar* situation that has nothing to do with the *current* situation you are in," he stretched his neck as he emphasized the words.

"Ladies, I've got news for you. Your husband isn't the father you strived so hard to receive emotional support from. You chose your husband based on an unhealthy 'comfortable' place and now you deal with the same feelings you had all those years growing up, and you're not getting the emotional support you so long to have."

He paused and said. "Not in this group, of course, but women in general."

Angela's cheeks were flushed and her eyes brimmed with tears. Linda just stared straight ahead as the team continued to walk.

"And guys are no different. We long to be accepted by our dads or parents and when we get passed over or rejected enough by our dad, we bury the pain, which ends up erupting later in workaholism, drug abuse, or affairs, to name a few. We start seeing issues with pride, fear, anger, doubt . . . you name it, and it all comes out some way.

"Guys, let it go, we can't get it back, and we'll never be able to make up that time. Forgive your dad, even if it isn't in your heart, and then let it go. Start realizing when these old feelings start happening and then STOP, recognize it's your hippocampus kicking in, and make a conscientious effort to . . . what?"

Everyone except Linda said in unison, "Change the thought, change the feeling, and change the action."

"We call this our—?"

"TFA!" shouted Abe

"Yep, TFA. Remember that. Thoughts, feelings, actions, or behavior. Let me share an example of this in my own life. Remember what I told you about how I had a career in finance and had an executive position? I shared about the drugs, the so called social drinking, affairs . . . all very real in my life. I was never mean or nasty, just—well, I avoided people as much as possible. I even avoided my wife, who knows me like a book. But I thought if I could avoid her, she wouldn't see the lie I was living.

"It was a constant battle, and before I knew it, I was involved with another woman. And believe me, I know it is not a 'before I knew it.' It was a slow process that I justified, every—step—of—the—way!" he enunciated each word sharply.

Stuart started to breathe heavily as he listened. Bile rose in his throat as he thought of having to someday face the lies he was living. *But I won't have to do that if I take care of things. Just find a decent cliff and make sure you finish the job.*

"And the truth will set you free," Joshua was saying when Stuart regained his focus. "Once I shared everything with my wife—I had to seriously repent. Joshua held his hand up as though he were going to shake someone's hand. "I had to turn 180 degrees," and he turned to face the group and walked backwards. "You turn from the behavior—180 degrees. You don't think about turning, you just do it. But you don't jump from zero to 180...you have to step through every degree of change to get to that 180 degree change.

"And so began a long, painful process of my repenting and my wife's role in forgiving me. But we made the decision together that we were going to fight for our marriage."

That's what's missing. We don't have the fight, and I'm not sure I want it anymore, Stuart thought.

"But every time I was a few minutes late, you can imagine what her hippocampus was going through and she would start having those old feelings and reactions! And every now and then I would slip back into fear and doubt and bury the feelings that would bubble up with those thoughts. And when that happened, I'd over compensate with pride, I would be OVERLY confident and extremely prideful. The next thing that would happen was my hippocampus would kick in telling me that 'I can do better. Someone else will appreciate me more,' and then that person would make me feel even more confident—it went on and on.

"But once my wife and I were committed to the marriage, we agreed that when those thoughts were generated, we're going to nip them in the bud immediately, before the feelings get stirred up. And for me that was really tough," he strained his neck. "I was in trouble deep so you cannot even imagine the pain we went through, my wife especially." His eyes dampened as he blinked and he turned to walk forward.

"We did a complete 180 degree turn, because we changed the thoughts, changed the feelings, and our behavior totally changed. We are not even the same people today, thank God! And we agreed to try and make a difference in each other's lives every day. We heard that if you do something consistently for 21 days in a row, or 30 to 40 repetitions, it will become a habit. By the same token if you **stop** doing something that you want to stop for 21 days that will become a habit. So we did," he smiled.

He pounded his stick and said, "Once again, we have arrived!" Joshua smiled as he opened his arms wide and welcomed the site of the cabins, their homestead. "Any questions before we take a break?"

Preston raised his hand. "I do have a question. The way you explained it, the process you went through with your wife seems so logical and matter of fact. First we did this, then we did that, and violá we are now changed. I don't imagine it was that methodical. This has to be a lot harder than you describe, am I right?"

"Preston, thanks for asking, and yes, it was and still is extremely hard. Many times we wanted to give up, but for me the pain of staying in an affair and then drinking to bury the pain…the pain of staying there was overwhelming. I could not stay there. The pain was crushing me. In fact, I actually thought of suicide; it actually made sense to me."

Stuart gulped hard as he listened intently.

"I needed to change so badly that I thought of ending my life. But then I took one single step, and actually uttered the dreaded words I needed to say, 'Honey, I need to share something with you.' And so the process began. I took one step at a time, a baby step, and then the next. I couldn't run a marathon, but I just did the next thing. A great theologian, Oswald Chambers, always said, 'do the next thing,' and Henry Blackaby went a bit further by saying, 'Never let the uncertainty of the second step keep you from taking the first step.'

> *We can change our*
> *Thoughts, Feelings, and Actions*

"We peeled away the pain and chipped away at our walls one step at a time. I went through the steps of a real, true genuine apology. I acknowledged what I did and I said I was wrong; I was truly sorry for my behavior. I then asked for forgiveness and I waited for an answer, which didn't immediately spill out of her mouth, let me tell you. That was the longest few minutes waiting for her to say yes or no. So I waited," he stopped and looked around. "And I waited. And when she finally answered yes. I asked that she hold me accountable to never do that again. That I never allow myself to get into a situation that even remotely opens the door to that temptation again.

"I also asked if she had anything else I need to repent for. And oh boy was there ever. And we've grown closer ever since. I'm not perfect by any means, but I have an awesome wife who loves me and is my best friend and bumper person. And I'll share what a bumper person is later.

"Dinner is same place, same time..."

Abe interrupted. "Hey Joshua do you mind if I pass out something?"

"No, Abe, I don't mind at all...by all means!" Joshua swept his arm out in front of him as though he were yielding the floor.

Abe handed everyone a bronze coin. "I knew you were all listening to me and Stuart talk about TFA—change the thought, feeling and action. I handed him a similar coin to remember the process of 'change' and inscribed on these T.F.A as well. Just a little token from me!"

"Thanks, Abe," everyone said as they flipped the coin over and examined it closer.

"Thanks, Abe," Joshua said as he nodded toward Abe. "That was mighty nice of you!" He turned his attention back to the group. "Okay, folks—dinner, same time, same place. We have one more 'step' to talk about in this whole process of TFAs, and we can do that over dinner if you are up for it."

Stuart started walking toward his cabin, still listening somewhat to Joshua, but lost in his own painful world. *His experience has nothing to do with me. I am in a totally different place, I don't drink, and I go to church...*

Stuart whipped around, expecting to see someone. "What?" he said aloud. He swatted at a swarm of bugs and stumbled over some stones on the path. He caught a glimpse of Linda watching him. He nervously wiped his mouth and started jogging toward the cabin, trying to maintain his composure.

Joshua clapped his hands and said, "See you all in about 30 minutes for dinner. Hey Stuart," he called out. "You okay buddy?"

Stuart reached for the wooden screen door. "I'm good," he replied, waving his other hand.

CHAPTER FIFTEEN:

Personal Growth

Stuart opened the screen door and ran into the bathroom and splashed cold water on his face. When he finally emerged, Frank was back in the cabin and avoided Stuart.

"If you're finished in there, I'll go ahead and clean up," Frank said timidly.

"Yeah, sure, go ahead." Stuart wiped his mouth with his hand and nodded.

Stuart lay on the bed, looking up at the cobweb in the corner of the ceiling. *What's going on? Why am I feeling this way? I need to get my act together and remember the only reason I came here was to end this craziness and find a cliff I can jump off. I get pulled into these crazy conversations of Joshua's and then we end up back here*—"Geez, I hate this," he said aloud as he sat up straight, breathing heavily. Frank quietly tip toed through the cabin, slowly walking out the door, not saying a word.

Stuart was sweating profusely as he ran his hands through his hair. "Maybe I'll just hang out for awhile," he said as he looked out the window, watching the others walking toward the gathering place.

"So, tell me something good!" Joshua started as everyone filled their plates and began eating. Everyone was quiet until Abe spoke. "It was a great hike today, and exhausting. I don't remember this leg of the hike being so difficult."

Everyone nodded and continued eating. Preston raised his hand as he swallowed a bite of food. "I finally understand the whole hippocampus thing along with change the thought, change the feeling, and change the action!"

"Yeah," Joshua beamed. "And how's it working for you?"

"I think it could change a lot of how I do things. I mean, who knew that some of my issues, or at least what I have been told are my issues," he raised his eyebrows, "could be because of my hippocampus? You're right, though," he tapped his forefinger to his chin. "There could be some freedom in this."

Joshua laughed. "It's not 'there could be,' man. There **is** freedom in this. So now that you know some of this information, have you ever thought about what you are willing to do that no one else in your industry or your community or your church is willing to do that can set you apart?"

Everyone stared and cocked their heads to one side or the other.

Frank spoke just above a whisper, "Get rid of our hippocampus stuff?"

"On the right track, Frank."

Joshua stuffed a forkful of food into his mouth and chewed, and waited.

"Get rid of our personal stuff or constraints that hold us back?" Angela asked sheepishly.

"Bingo," Joshua pointed his fork in the air, accentuating the point.

Preston and Doug both raised their hands but Preston spoke first. "We can't affect other people's personal constraints that end up binding us, so it seems pointless to try to do that!"

Joshua said, "Exactly. So, why do we even bother getting frustrated with other people when we cannot be responsible for whatever it is they are doing? We are only responsible for our own thoughts, feelings, and actions and any personal constraint that gets in our way."

"Isn't that a bit self-centered, Joshua?" asked Linda.

"Great question, Linda. Why would you consider that self-centered?" asked Joshua.

"Well," she looked to the side. "We're supposed to be all about helping others and being more concerned about others..." Linda stopped in mid sentence as Stuart walked into the dining area.

Joshua turned to look in the direction Linda was looking. "Hey, Stuart, glad you're here. Grab a plate and heap some of that good cookin' from the steaming pan over there. We'll wait, right gang?" He smiled as he looked around at everyone.

Stuart stirred around a couple of pieces of chicken. Then realizing everyone was watching him, he picked up a piece and some silverware and turned to sit down by Abe.

"Okay, so Linda, why do you think it's self-centered when I said we are not responsible for what other people do?"

"Like I said," she crossed her legs and turned away from Joshua. "We're supposed to be all about helping others. So, if someone we love is behaving poorly, isn't it our responsibility to point out that bad behavior?" she said as she noticed and picked up a piece of lint off Frank's shirt.

"So, if you **lovingly** point out to a **loved** one," Joshua emphasized the love words, "a behavior that could be deemed offensive, does that make you actually responsible for that loved one's behavior?"

"Well, uh, no, but aren't you supposed to help them with changing that behavior? Linda asked as she struggled to understand."

"I suppose," responded Joshua. "But how do you help them?"

"Well," Linda twisted in her chair and held her hands up. "You point it out, you tell them, and you're specific about their actions. I just think it's self-centered to say, 'Oh well, I'm not responsible for how badly you behave!'"

"You're making two different points, Linda." Joshua's tone changed as he lowered his voice and looked directly into Linda's eyes. She lowered her eyes to look at her nails. "When you care about someone and they do something that has offended you, you go to them and talk directly about the issue and specifically about how it relates to your feelings. Many times when a friend or a loved one points something out to me, it opens my eyes to a behavior I had no idea I was doing. So that's one point!

"But, once I become aware of it, is it my friend's responsibility to see that my thoughts change, or that my feelings change, and then ultimately that my behavior changes?" Joshua explained.

Everyone shook their heads slowly side to side—except Linda.

"They can check on me to see how I am doing with a new response or behavior, but they can't possibly do it for me. Only I can make those changes."

Joshua looked around at everyone. Quietly he asked, "Make sense?"

Everyone nodded.

Grace rocked back on her heels as she spoke up. "You bring up a good point. We hit on something before about constraints. Any idea how you can break through a personal constraint, or, in my case, many personal constraints," she beamed as her eyes bounced in contagious joy.

Doug responded confidently, "Change the thought, change the feeling, and change the action!"

Joshua laughed, "Yep, but now let's drill down a bit deeper. Are you up for it?"

"Yes!" came the resounding response from the whole group.

"So, a great way to remove personal constraints, and we all have them, is to commit to growing personally. But where do we begin?"

The silence returned. But this time it was more like a comforting blanket that allowed the group to take time and think, to process and not jump on a first reaction. The looks on their faces made it clear that they were becoming more comfortable with the silence and were able to breathe in a fresh perspective.

"My story is a perfect example." Stuart watched Grace take a seat and lean back with a gleam in her eyes. *The group is beginning to "get it," and it must feel pretty darn good to Grace and Joshua. But I feel like I am swimming in this murky dark crud.* Stuart felt like he was in a tar pit—the overwhelming sense of failure was clouding his vision even as he watched Grace beam more and more. The dark voice was all he knew and he began to despise Grace and Joshua and their ability to rise above their problems, *or, as they say, 'constraints'.*

"So, the rest of the story is this," she said softly. "After reconnecting with Suzy's family, I felt that I had learned my lesson. I was really careful about the things I did. In fact, I didn't drive when I drank. But I continued to be a party girl. We would designate somebody to stay sober so they could drive—this was before the term designated driver ever came into our vocabulary—and the rest of us partied.

"Funny I was never the designated driver. I didn't learn until much later that it was because I was never sober. Now you would think that someone who killed their best friend while driving drunk would never drink again, right? Well, I didn't drink, I would just have a sip here and there, I never had a beer in my hand, I just drank everyone else's beer. I never bought marijuana, I just smoked everyone else's. You get the picture.

"Everyone started into their career and while I was really blessed to have a decent job, I was going nowhere. I had to take a really hard look at myself—What was I doing, how could I be drinking like that??" Grace stood and limped a bit as she straightened up. "I was a mess, and for some reason, no one really loved me enough to say anything to me. Everybody buried their head in the sand thinking they didn't want to upset me. I needed help.

"So I joined AA."

Everyone leaned back, some with a surprised look!

"That's right, I had to take a look at myself and commit to making a change. But the initial time I was with AA, I thought, "These people are losers. I am not that bad!

"I found out real quick, I was the only one who had been charged with reckless homicide and served time for it. So who's the loser now?"

Grace stopped and rested back against the table as she took in a deep breath.

"I saw the mess I was, I committed to make a change by attending AA and now it was time to actually make a behavior change, but I went kicking. I could stand there and say, 'Hi, I'm Grace and I'm an alcoholic,' but I wasn't ready to give up drinking. That would mean no longer hanging out with my friends and I wasn't ready to do that.

"After a few months of attending the group, I realized that if my friends could not help me stop drinking, they were probably not my friends. Little by little though they started coming alongside and doing activities that did not involve drinking and it became easier to not drink. I didn't realize how silly people were when they drink." She shrugged and smiled.

"I've been clean for 16 years," she said somberly. "It was a tough journey, to say the least. Realizing I was an alcoholic was devastating for me. I then committed to make a change and did a 180 degrees turn with my behavior. I'm in a great place now. My family is a lot happier as well knowing I have gone through so much healing. It was a difficult process but the steps I took were incredible for my personal growth."

Angela spoke, "Wow, you really have to keep an open mind that once you see something within yourself that is a constraint, or causing problems with your relationships—you stop that behavior," Angela waved her hands in the air as she shook her head and smiled. "I don't think I can do that. I'm not sure I even want to take a look at myself like that."

Joshua smiled and joined in the conversation, "I think you probably can, in fact I know you can," he said as he stood up, put his hands in his pockets, and then took a couple of steps to stretch. "Perhaps it helps us if we have folks in our life who shine a light on the areas where we need personal evaluation. Did you hear Grace say that no one in her family loved her enough to let her know her life was out of control?   Often, we are totally blind to our internal flaws so many times it's our kids, our spouse, friends, or God who share the truth with us. It's whoever is honest and loves us enough to tell us we've got lettuce in our teeth. How many times have you gone home after being out all day and noticed you had a piece of lettuce in your teeth, a wardrobe malfunction, or some other physical mishap and no one told you? And, if you were to ask them why they didn't, what would be their answer? 'I didn't want to embarrass you.' So, letting me walk around with lettuce in my teeth was not embarrassing?"

Everyone laughed out loud in acknowledgement of the truth.

"I was at a luncheon with some friends and a few folks from my church. I sat right next to the pastor's wife, who was as sweet and gentle as they come. She'd walk into a room and it would just fill up with sweetness.

"Anyway, she and I started talking and she smiled and…BAM. Right there in the middle of her gorgeous smile is a big ol' piece of lettuce. So I leaned over and whispered, 'Anita, you've got a piece of lettuce in your teeth.' So she took a napkin," he said as he demonstrated discreetly getting a piece of lettuce out of his teeth. "She smiled and I nodded my head and winked."

"A few minutes later we're enjoying ourselves, talking, relaxing, and Anita laughed in her usual sweet way and wouldn't you know it," he smiled as he pointed to his teeth. Everyone chuckled, anticipating what may come. "So once again, I leaned over and whispered, 'Anita, I hate to tell you this but you have another piece of lettuce stuck in your teeth.' Well, this time, as she got it out she could not help but smile ever so sweetly. Anita turned to me and said, 'Joshua, you must love me an awful lot to be able to tell me that two times in a row. Thank you!' So, ever since then, anytime we need to refer to letting someone know about an issue or problem we say, 'You've got lettuce in your teeth.'"

Joshua clapped his hands and rubbed them together. "Everybody good?"

Everyone nodded.

"Okay, so we'll wrap this part up because we have an awesome way to 'launch' our evening together."

Stuart took in a deep breath and grabbed his glass of water. *I hope we go late tonight. I vote for less time in the cabin in the dark.* He took three big gulps of water as he closed his eyes.

Grace stood up with her trusty goodie bag. They knew they were in for a special treat when she had her hand in the bag. "Since we were talking about someone pointing out or shining a light on a character flaw, a bad behavior, a problem or issue, whether it's lettuce in our teeth," she gave a wink, "or being greedy or even cheating on a spouse— Stuart choked on his water and leaned forward. Abe gently patted him on the back, leaned over and asked, "You okay, brother?"

Stuart just nodded

Grace continued. "I have a tool…doesn't look like much of a tool though, I'll admit." She threw small compact mirrors to everyone. "Keep them in your bag. You just never know when you might need to check yourself for spinach in your teeth—and do a little self-evaluation!"

Stuart wiped his mouth and coughed, pretending he had swallowed the wrong way. *Is there some way that people know I might be cheating on my wife? They probably do know and are judging me in their oh so subtle way. God, everyone probably knows now except my wife, Jill.*

Oh, don't kid yourself, said the dark voice. *She's known all along. She's known every time you've had an affair.* Stuart put his hands over his ears as if to stop hearing the voice. *That's why this plan has to work, remember? You have to see it through because it is the only way she will forgive you, once you're gone. Just think, at the funeral, they'll all be saying nice things about you and she'll forget all the times she wondered where you were and who you were with and she'll be convinced you were indeed a good husband and father. And you didn't have to do a thing but,"* the voice lowered and seemed to slither around Stuart's neck as it whispered, *"finish the job."*

Stuart shook his head and held his ears.

> ***Steps for Personal Growth***
> **Personal Evaluation: See it.** *Looking inside is more difficult that looking outside. Acknowledge that a constraint exists. Get a clue: {Thoughts}*
>
> **Take Control: Own it.** *Accept responsibility and exercise control over it. Get a grip: {Feelings}*
>
> **Change Direction or redirect:** *Change it! A commitment to action. Get a life: {Actions Or Behaviors}*

Joshua stopped talking and looked at Stuart. "Stuart, you okay, man?"

"Yeah, must just be something with the altitude. Not sure but keep going, this is good stuff." He mustered up as much normalcy as he possibly could.

And in the silent moment when all eyes were on him, he focused on the concerned look on Joshua's face, Stuart heard, *Just do the next thing, just take the next step. Don't look too far ahead, and don't dwell on the past. Just be in the present moment.*

Joshua nodded as he continued. "So, we shine a light on a behavior problem. When we recognize we have a constraint, a flaw, a problem—wow! Talk about freedom. You know, for some time before we acknowledge the problem, we have this self-talk going on in our head constantly. We'll hear one time, 'Oh go ahead. It won't hurt anyone.' Then the next time we hear, 'but what about your family,' or 'are you really being honest by padding that expense report?'"

Frank lifted his chin and said, "Yeah, sort of like the cartoons back in the day that had an angel on one shoulder and the devil on the other. One would be the good side, and the other was the bad."

Everyone smiled and nodded in agreement.

Stuart was quiet as he pondered the 'conversation' he had just had in his head.

"Exactly, Frank," said Joshua. "And even though one was good and the other was bad, do you remember how they were depicted? One was perceived as much more 'fun' while the other was boring. Which one was which?"

"Oh, the good was always boring."

"Yeah—oh those subtle messages. But let me tell you folks—those conversations are very real. Are Frank and I the only ones who have ever experienced this?" he asked as he held up his right hand.

Everyone held up a hand except Linda, who was doodling instead of paying attention, and Stuart, who though he was staring at Joshua, seemed also to be in another place.

Joshua looked around somberly and in just above a whisper said, "And don't discount that you have an enemy that would like nothing more than to see you get off track."

Silence. This time it was just uncomfortable enough for the team to really reflect on his words and their meaning.

A thunderous clap of Joshua's hands brought them back to the discussion.

"Okay, let's keep going. Once you accept responsibility and acknowledge a bad behavior, exercise control over it, then you redirect your behavior. Remember, it doesn't mean walking around in ashes and sackcloth and moping around saying, "Oh woe is me," all the time. It is the actual turning from the mindset and behavior that caused us to get off track and interfere with our relationships—and folks, if you haven't figured it out by now . . . it is all about relationships. Whether you're a salesman, a CEO, an IT tech, a pastor, a mom or dad—it is all about relationships.

"The most successful people are not the ones who are smartest or prettiest or richest—it's the ones who can have true, genuine, and authentic relationships. The more you can shine a light on your own personal constraints and break through them, the more genuine and successful you will be in your relationships and in your business."

Joshua raised his eyes slightly past the team and said, "Everyone, grab a dessert and we'll finish this topic and head into our evening activity, if you are up to it." He stopped and looked up.

Stuart turned and looked over his shoulder and saw a tray full of crystal glasses filled with rich, creamy filling layered between fresh blueberries and ripe, red strawberries. Stuart quickly looked around, hoping to see a car, jeep, bicycle, or any other sign of a human being. "How on earth do you do that?"

"You have to think way beyond the box, Stuart—or, as we say—way beyond the bubble," Joshua said as he picked up a glass. He dipped his spoon into it and pulled out a juicy red berry swimming in creamy deliciousness. Once everyone had a dessert, or, in Doug's case, two, Joshua stopped eating and asked, "So, the question is, will you accept what you 'see' through personal evaluation and change what needs to change by taking control and then changing direction?"

No one said a word, but most nodded and pretended to concentrate on their dessert. "So how is this coming together for you?" Joshua asked.

Doug took one last lick of his spoon and said, "Not sure I am really getting all this. Like my name says, I am doubtful, but I'll give this a shot by sharing a scenario I recently experienced. I had been given a leadership position with a cross-divisional team. I followed our company's protocol to a tee, but the team wasn't functioning; we were just not getting the job done. I immediately went to that place of, 'It's me, I can't do it, and I'm a failure . . .' Well, one of my coworkers, who is a really caring person, came to me and said, 'You've laid everything out, you've given the goals of what is expected of the team and our purpose, but when we complete an action, it is never to your satisfaction. So we never know what you personally expect from us, and, unfortunately, we always seem to disappoint you.'

"Wow. I thought that was really out of left field. At the time though, I thanked her, my real thought process was, 'I *have* been clear, but if *you* would just work harder and if *you* would meet the goals I've laid out for the team, we'd get it done.' Needless to say, I didn't accept what that person was telling me.

"Looking back, I can see the behavior I was engaged in. In my head, I actually did put additional levels of expectations on my team. I never told them or shared with them what those expectations were, and when they didn't meet them, I exploded."

Doug looked down at his hands as he continued to speak. "Understanding what I do now about hippocampus and how it feeds my behavior, I can really see how that affects all we do." Doug's face lit up like a child who figured out the secret code on the back of the cereal box.

"How's that, Doug?" asked Joshua.

"Well, I grew up with the same kind of 'hidden agendas.' When I was told to go make my bed, I would make it to the best of my ability with what I knew, and when that wasn't good enough, I got yelled at. How was I supposed to know what a good job looked like without being given clear direction or being told all that is expected of me—or shown—you know, the 'involve me' part of learning? And yet that is exactly how I treated my team members. I didn't give them all the details or direction and then got upset with them when they didn't do it right."

Joshua stared at Doug for a moment and then nodded his head. He said, "You never know where the 'acknowledgement' will come from. The question is, are we open to that acknowledgement or feedback? Doug, thank you! That was a great example. What do you think would have happened had you been open to that feedback from your team member at the time she gave it?"

Doug leaned his head back, rolled a toothpick around in his mouth, and said slowly, "I suppose I would have stepped back and taken time to personally assess my behavior."

"Just like you did here," jumped in Joshua. "Then what?"

"I would have taken control. I would have stopped doing what I was doing and then redirected that behavior. I would have taken the time to give clear direction and involve the team step by step until I knew they understood. And the team I was overseeing would have been wildly successful," he said with a smile.

Joshua beamed and said, "Well done!"

Stuart listened and watched the volley back and forth between Joshua and Doug, but had a hard time focusing on what they were saying. It was beginning to get dark, and all he could think about was how he was going to stay awake all night so he wouldn't have to face the dark again.

CHAPTER SIXTEEN:

Acknowledging Anger and Fear

Joshua looked at the moon as it brightened and the surrounding sky darkened. He grabbed another dish of dessert and said, "Let's move to the fire pit. Feel free to bring your desserts if you're not quite finished or would like more."

Everyone else left their empty dessert dishes and followed Joshua. He walked briskly over a small, lighted gravel path, down a slightly sloping grassy hill and then hopped over a small stone wall to an open area. There were eight large cushioned beach chairs nestled up against the stone wall that Joshua hopped over. He turned around and reached out his hand to help Grace step over the wall. In the middle of the semi circle of beach chairs was a large red brick pit. A roaring fire danced in the center, and sparks of embers spiraled upward and crackled with pops that sounded in harmony with the crickets. Everyone found a comfortable chair and snuggled into it. Joshua opened a sack that held eight large wooden sticks and a huge bag of marshmallows.

As Stuart settled in, he felt a sense of comfort he had not felt in some time. Everyone seemed so delighted with the chairs, the fire, and the very real possibility of having toasted marshmallows. All of a sudden his eyes widened. He caught his breath as he looked just beyond the fire pit and over the crest of the mountainside. Far below their resting place was a valley with a small village area. The lights of the homes and businesses were slowly beginning to illuminate, giving the surrounding area a warm glow.

Joshua stood near the edge of the pit, smiling with a glimmer in his eyes as he watched the team enjoying themselves. "Okay, everyone comfortable?"

Everyone nodded.

"Great!" he said as he looked in the direction of Linda, who was directing Frank to put something under her feet.

Stuart watched Joshua intently as he passed out the sticks and marshmallows.

Preston extended his marshmallow-clad stick over the fire and watched it soften on the inside and melt into crispy brown bubbling sugar on the outside.

As the sun continued to descend behind a mountain, the air took on a chill, and one by one everyone cuddled up in the blanket that was folded and waiting over the backs of the chairs. Joshua stood quietly to observe. He had that familiar hint of a smile on his face while he silently stood by to see the interaction of the group.

Angela stared into the fire and with a monotone voice, said, "This reminds me of my dad."

"Why's that, Angela?" asked Joshua.

She came out of her trance-like stare and smiled. "Oh, when I was a kid, we would grill on summer nights and go into the back yard, grab some long twigs and roast marshmallows while the coals were still hot. It was a blast." She stared back into the fire. "Can I share about something about my dad?"

Joshua nodded.

"Well," she kept her eyes focused on the flames, "in my home I have a flag and some medals and some documents. They belonged to my dad when he was in the military. Anyway, I have the flag that was laid over his coffin. It's nicely folded, in a wooden and glass case. The medals are all on top of the flag, all carefully placed in the case. I keep it right in my living room, I see it every day, and I think about him every time I pass it."

She lowered her head and swallowed hard. She looked up, took in a deep breath and blew it out. "I am the youngest in my family and I am a lot younger that my next sibling in line. So I was almost an only child and clearly a surprise to my mom and dad," she laughed. "But my dad," her voice broke, "was my hero. And I didn't even know about his days serving our country when I was young. He would do all sorts of things with me, but the most memorable times were when he would have tea with me." Her eyes spilled over with tears as she tried to continue. Frank got up and gave her a tissue.

Angela dabbed her eyes. "Anyway, my dad would have tea parties with me. He'd sit in a chair and we'd have imaginary scones and delicious fruity tea. He had this way of describing the food and drinks that made me believe we had the best tea party of any girl in the neighborhood. He made me feel so good all the time, about my grades, about any project, about anything I did—he built my confidence. My mom did too, but man, when it came from my dad—I was soaring.

"So, my dad died when I was eight years old." She let out a quiet sob, wiped her eyes again, and then blew her nose. Joshua gave her a small packet of tissues. "I know that was a very long time ago," she laughed nervously, "but it still hurts like it was yesterday." She sniffed as she looked at Joshua, "Guess that's some of my hippocampus stuff, uh?"

Joshua nodded and warmly smiled.

Angela continued. "When I came home one day from school, I walked in and my aunt and uncle were there and my mom was crying, and then my mom had to tell me he had died in an accident. I couldn't believe it. And of course, in my parents' generation, you never show emotion. We all just had to suck it up. I mean we were sad, but we never really were allowed to show how sad we felt.

"I was eight years old and I remember every moment," she sniffed. "I was so angry that my dad died so soon—I had no way to deal with my anger, my sadness. I was so upset and no one reached out to help in any way. So that's how I learned to pretty much handle my grief—in angry outbursts. I grew up, went through a couple of failed marriages, and now I just focus all my energy on my career. I realized that no one I married, or even dated for that matter, could ever live up to my dad. And I just got angrier.

"So," she wiped her eyes with a tissue, "being on this hike and learning these things, I am starting to realize how that event and the emotions that went with it really affect my life to this day!" She nodded her head and whispered, "Wow, I wasn't really planning on sharing all that but—it just came out." She let out a little laugh as she wiped her nose. "And it actually felt pretty good to share."

"Thanks, Angela," said Joshua, quietly. Stuart sat with his mouth opened—amazed that Angela's whole countenance softened.

Frank raised his hand, "Are we sharing memories?"

Joshua shrugged his shoulders. "You can share whatever is on your mind or nothing if you just want to sit quietly and enjoy this magnificent view."

"Well, I would like to share something—Angela made me think about my grandma. I'll never forget this—she was one tough cookie," he chuckled. "Anyway, she was a typical grandma, and she lived a couple of blocks from us. So I was able to walk over there and just hang out with her while she baked or cooked. She would teach me all sorts of things because she must have enjoyed her time with me.

"She was my dad's mom. Well, I grew up with this god-awful fear of my dad, and for good reason," he shifted his eyes to the left. "Well, one day we were all over at my grandma's house and I did something—who knows what. But I was a little kid. Well, my dad got up to come after me and my grandma stood right in front of him and said, 'You lay one hand on that child and I'll take you round back and whip you, boy.' My dad sat down and didn't come after me—at least not in front of grandma. Seems my dad was scared to death of grandma," he looked at Joshua. "My grandma died a few years ago but I just had a flash of that memory. She was this little tiny thing and she stood up to my dad who towered over her—wow! Wish I could have done that. I was never able to stand up to my dad. And as tough as he was, he didn't do much to protect me, either"

Linda squirmed in her chair, stared into the fire, and did not say a word.

Joshua watched Frank and waited.

Preston raised his hand. "I'd like to share something." He coughed to clear his throat and stretched his neck. "I have this old baseball mitt at home, packed away, but every now and then I'll get it out, rub some oil in it, and soften it up." He opened his hand and rubbed his palm with his other hand. "My dad loved to play baseball." He pretended to throw a baseball. He chuckled under his breath and looked down. "But I hated baseball. Believe it or not, I preferred to study or read and I was much better with numbers. I know, sounds boring, but I was fascinated with numbers games, puzzles that made me really think. In fact, I was 7 years old when I pretended to open my first checking account and started helping kids in the neighborhood start their own businesses. Ha, that's a great memory." He threw his head back and laughed aloud.

"Yeah, well, anyway," he said somberly, "As much as I hated sports, I played catch with my dad, just because I wanted to be with him," He shrugged. "Anyway, I am quite proud of my past but that was probably too much information, right?"

Joshua slowly shook his head, "Not at all."

Doug jumped in, "Preston, I know exactly what you mean. In fact, I have my mom's recipe book that I hold onto just for memory sake. Man, I remember all the way back to when I was two and would sit on the kitchen counter and watch my mom cook. And my dad, as well. He loved being in the kitchen. They had the best time cooking together, and I can remember watching and my mom would say, 'Dougie, can you give me the salt?' And she'd point to the saltshaker and I would give it to her. It was my way of being with my mom and I loved cooking with her.

"But the kids in the neighborhood thought I was a sissy," he winced as he spoke. "So I played sports," he sniffed and then laughed as he looked at Preston.

"But I grew up loving the art of cooking and would love to take a professional course. But for now, I enjoy cooking for my family and they seem to really enjoy my creations." His face lit up as he smiled and nodded toward Joshua.

"Wow," said Joshua. "I think Doug loves to cook! Anyone else get that feeling? Thanks for sharing!"

"Josh, you may have heard this before so I apologize. I have an old rosary," Abe said as he pulled it out of his pocket. "I carry it everywhere with me. You see, my dad..." Abe hung his head as he shook the rosary back and forth. He looked up. "Dad was just a flat out mean drunk. He'd beat on me every chance he had. God knows how many times he beat on Mama."

Stuart's mouth dropped opened as he listened intently to his friend. He lowered his head, as he shook it from side to side. He never realized the similar paths he and Abe had growing up. Abe tried to share with him and get him to open up but Stuart kept his distance.

"As hard as it was, I left my home when I was really young. Years later, I tried reconnecting with my mom, but I learned she had passed." His voice was shaky, "Didn't even get to say goodbye," he said through pursed lips as his chin quivered.

"So my aunt, she's the one I connected with, she told me my dad was dying. I didn't care much. In fact I thought, let him die. But day after day after day, the thought of him being an old worn out man dying alone just gnawed at me. So I found out where he was and went to visit. He recognized me right away. He looked like a dying old man would look after living the life he had.

"But his face lit up best it could when he saw me. I didn't say anything. Just sat down across from his bed and stared at him. Finally he said how sorry he had been, how he wished he could have said he was sorry to Mama but she died before he made some changes in his life.

"Seems he found Jesus so he said he was at peace with dying. Then he looked me in the eyes with a look I had never seen from him. And he said, 'Son, I don't like knowing how I treated you and your mama.' My pa started crying like a baby. I had never seen that before. He kept going, 'Before I go see my maker, I need to know something. Will you forgive me for all those things I did to you?'

"Well, no way could I forgive him. I was amazed he would ask, but I was so full of anger when I was staring at him that I just shook my head no. It was like my revenge on him. Yep, I finally got him.

"But he just looked at me and said he understood. In fact, he said he didn't blame me. Then he asked me to pull out this box on his bed stand. That box held this rosary, which is funny in itself because my family was southern Baptist. But he explained to me that his dad had given it to him as a reminder of the forgiveness he needed. I didn't take it. I just walked out of the room.

"When he passed, the hospital gave me his things, and the rosary was still there. I took that and threw away the other things. Every day I would take that rosary and ask God to help me forgive him because I was so angry and hurt. I was imprisoned with anger and was unforgiving for years. One day it finally hit me. I am the one who has the power to forgive my father or remain bound with hate," he looked over at Grace who smiled warmly. "I was the one imprisoned with the hateful feelings I had. I finally let that anger go. So today and every day, I carry this rosary around to remind me of the power of forgiveness. It is so freeing. If you just change the thought…"

Angela and Frank dabbed their eyes while Stuart stared into the fire with a faraway look. A bullfrog and other creatures could be heard singing their nightly concert of sounds. The comfortable silence that blanketed everyone rolled in like a morning fog and waited.

"Thanks buddy," said Joshua.

Linda slowly raised her hand. "I think I'd like to share, if I could," she said quietly."

Joshua nodded.

"I had a really doting dad, too, Angela. He's still alive today, thank God." She dabbed her eyes. "My mom was very controlling—nice as could be, sugary sweet to everybody, but controlling and manipulative all the way. She passed away about 10 years ago. But my dad—as loving as he was, he wasn't around a lot but neither were any other dads in the neighborhood, so I figured that was pretty much how dads were." Her shrug seemed a veiled attempt to hide any pain.

"Well, at the age of 16, I fell in love and decided I wanted to be married. So my boyfriend at the time—not Frank—and I ran away to get married. Plus I was pregnant, go figure! My parents of course came after us, found us in the next town over and well of course all hell broke loose. They were mortified. Then when they found out I was pregnant..." she shook her head slowly side to side.

"My dad—my loving, doting dad—was so upset and heartbroken. My mom said I would either have an abortion or I would have to go away somewhere to have the baby and no one must ever know—didn't want to embarrass her, you know! I chose the abortion but my dad was never the same. I thought we could go back to being the way we were but that didn't happen. I'm all my dad has now but I can't help but see the look of disgust when he looks at me. I hate that look. I work really hard at making sure no one ever looked at me with disgust again."

Stuart felt a pang of sadness for Linda as he watched her face. She looked like a little girl, missing her daddy. It was more than he could take! After several minutes of silence, Stuart looked down and placed his hands on his knees and stood. "I think I'll retire. I'm not feeling well." With that, he turned and walked slowly back to the cabin, desperately trying not to let anyone see him shake as he stepped into the thick blanket of darkness. The clouds covered the luminous sky that had shined so brightly the evening before. He quickened his pace to make it back safely. As he reached the steps of the cabin, he heard the crunch of branches as though something heavy had stepped out of the woods. Stuart stopped; not wanting to draw attention to himself but his breathing was so heavy he felt he could be heard in the next county. He caught his breath and stared straight ahead. He felt something else was near him—or was it his imagination again?

He heard another crunch and jumped three steps and onto the porch. He almost pulled the screen door off the hinges as he ran into the cabin, slamming the door behind him. But he did not feel any safer inside than he did out in the dark. He turned on the only light in the cabin, but still could not catch his breath. So, he leaned against a wall, trying to convince himself that he was safe from anything outside that might be trying to kill him. He slowly started to chuckle, then laugh, and began laughing out loud. He was on the ground laughing so hard he was afraid he would not get up. So he turned over on his side and just lay there.

I am such an idiot. I come on a trip just to kill myself and I run away from my imagination? Yeah, he laughed under his breath. Then he stretched his neck, rolled his shoulders a bit to each side hoping to loosen the tight feeling, but he still was not able to shake the overwhelming feeling he was being watched.

He finally stood, walked into the bathroom, and splashed water on his face. He took his time as he brushed his teeth. Then he slowly, almost methodically walked toward the bed. He decided to stay in his clothes. Finally, he felt safe enough and lay on the bed desperately wanting to drift off to sleep. But then remembered…Frank would be coming. He no sooner had thought about him coming when Frank walked in the door and headed toward his bed. Without saying a word, he began taking his shoes off and crawling under the covers without even looking in the direction of Stuart's bed.

Stuart waited until Frank was snoring loudly and then silently slid out of his bed. He sat in the chair and pulled his knees up to his chest, struggling not to shake. He peered out the window and watched the moonbeams, which he imagined turned into some sort of strange creature. His fear enveloped him like a slithering snake and began to squeeze the life out of him.

He took in a deep, jagged gasp of air and opened his mouth to yell and wake up Frank. Nothing came out. He could feel his lungs fill and his stomach tighten as he tried and tried to yell for help, but still no sound. It was as though he were in a nightmare.

Stuart's heart started pounding and his breath grew shallow as his eyes darted back and forth. Frank was still snoring, but Stuart imagined there was another presence in the room. He quickly turned. Stuart gulped and let out a loud guttural scream as he backed up and tipped over the only lamp in the room.

Frank jumped out of bed and without even looking, bolted out of the cabin, slamming the screen door behind him. Just as quickly as Frank ran out, Joshua and Abe charged into the cabin. Joshua's flashlight searched the room and found Stuart screaming and cowering in the corner, pointing to the opposite side of the cabin.

"Over there, there on that side, see it, there it is. See it?"

Abe walked quietly over to his friend, patting him on the shoulder. "Stuart, it's me, Abe. You okay, buddy? What's going on? Tell me about it. What's happening?"

Stuart was pointing and yelling, "Don't look at me, get that thing! Look right over there, my God, can't you see what I'm talking about?" When Joshua shone the light where Stuart was pointing, they saw nothing.

"My God, right in that spot over there; I can feel something. Couldn't you feel it when you walked in here?" Stuart's face was red and a vein on the left side of his head was pulsating. He stood and paced back and forth as Joshua's light searched the room.

"Tell me what happened," Joshua asked calmly.

Stuart was flushed and somewhat embarrassed. His nostrils flared, "I know you think I'm crazy, I can tell. I saw this thing, I can't even tell you what it was. I don't know, maybe some sort of animal or creature. But it seemed to slither rather than walk, but it wasn't on the ground," he shrugged. "I don't know," he rubbed his fingers through his hair, "Maybe I *am* nuts. But something was in here, it was here, I saw it, I felt it." he panted as he motioned toward his own eyes.

Joshua and Abe looked at each other, and Stuart stopped and looked at them.

Anger is caused by:
Fear, Frustration or Pain
(Physical or emotional)!

"Go ahead, say it. I am certifiably nuts, right? Isn't that what the two of you are thinking?" Stuart yelled. Joshua reached out and put his hand on Stuart's shoulder, but Stuart quickly brushed it away and continued pacing. He wiped his brow.

"Stuart, listen, man, we really believe you, but try to settle down so we can get some facts and figure this out. Now just take a deep breath. Please, buddy, try and take a deep breath," Joshua inhaled as though he was trying to do it for Stuart.

Stuart smacked Joshua's hand away. "Look, it is not every day I witness something like this and you guys don't need to patronize me, so go on and get out of here. Go on!" His neck strained as he spit out the words.

Joshua said calmly, "We're not going anywhere, Stuart. We know that you are telling us the truth and we want to help sort through this. We want to figure out what's happening here."

"Joshua, I am not in the mood for one or your lessons. Just leave me alone!"

"Okay, my friend. We're just outside if you need us, right Abe?"

"You bet."

They both walked slowly toward the door. As they looked back, Stuart was staring out the window. They closed the door. The rest of the team, except Linda, was right outside of the door. Joshua asked that they all go back to bed and try to get a good night's sleep. Frank quietly walked back into the cabin and crawled into bed.

"What happened in there?" Abe asked.

"I'm not sure, but it seemed pretty real to him. He seems really scared—and very angry. Only one of three things would cause him to get so angry: fear, frustration, or pain." Joshua turned to look at Abe. "You know pretty him well. Is he in some sort of emotional or physical pain, is he frustrated, or afraid of something? What is it?"

"Yeah, I do know him well, and I have to say it is all three—although you wouldn't know it just by talking to him."

"I don't know, Abe. I picked that up from him in the first two minutes. He is a very confused man and very scared about something. Maybe he's worried about losing 'all he's worked for' and frustrated because he is constantly hiding an 'unacceptable behavior', thinking he's getting away with it. Ironically, it's the very thing he is hiding that is causing him pain. Yeah, it's definitely emotional pain but probably some physical pain now, don't you think? So what is he hiding?"

Abe shrugged his shoulders and shook his head. The two men reached their tents but continued talking as they looked back at Stuart's cabin. They could see the outline of his face as he stood silently staring out the window.

"Good question," Abe sighed. "I don't want to go with my gut just yet. I need some time to think about this and pray about it."

Joshua pulled the flap of his tent open and crawled in. He poked his head through the tent opening and said, "You'd better get to thinking and praying about it quick, because what I saw happen in there tonight, there's not a lot of time left, my friend!"

Abe turned to look at the cabin. The full moon cast a strange shadow over the meadow. Instead of entering his tent, Abe sat on a large rock to keep watch.

Frank pulled the covers over his head, and turned on his side, ignoring Stuart. Stuart shuddered as he turned to peer out the window. He could see the shadowy silhouette of Abe, and he knew his friend was praying. Stuart sat in the chair next to the window, let out a long sigh, pulled the blanket over him and held it tight under his chin, determined to stay awake and alert.

CHAPTER SEVENTEEN:

A Glorious Morning

The dew glistened on the grass as Frank and Stuart made their way to breakfast in silence. Everyone stopped what they were saying or doing as Stuart walked in with his head down.

"Morning', guys!" smiled Grace. Stuart nodded to her and then looked in Joshua's direction who was busy on his laptop.

"Heard you had a pretty dreadful night last night, big guy," said Linda to Stuart as she moved closer to Frank. "Good morning, husband," she smiled coyly.

"Sooooo, somebody tell me something good," Grace said melodically!

"The sun is up," smiled Frank.

"Yep, that is a great thing. Ahhh, the Creator made the sun come up just for us." Grace giggled and looked up, basking in the glimmer of sunrise that was brimming over the mountain. "What else?"

"Food is WONDERFUL!" said Angela.

"I don't know about anyone else, but I am actually learning a ton," said Preston.

"You sound surprised," Grace said, turning to Preston.

"Frankly, I am." He arched his eyebrows and laughed.

Abe walked in quietly and poured a cup of coffee. He went over to sit next to Stuart and patted him on the shoulder. He didn't say a word.

"Well, good," Grace said as she smiled. "Perhaps there'll be more to learn today. Before we go on, I have a tool for you." She handed out a gift card and everyone was excitedly reaching out to grab the card.

"Uh," grunted Frank as he read the card.

Grace laughed, "What do you see, Frank?"

"A gift card for The Hiking Shoppe?" He turned the card, "Wait, it says specifically for a pair of hiking boots, right?"

"Yep, does anyone want to guess why this is significant?"

Joshua turned from his netbook to observe the group activity. Everyone was silent.

"Oh, oh—I get it!" said Frank as he waved the card. "The tool for Personal Growth—this is for the *steps* for personal growth, right? The hiking shoes represent the steps we need to take for personal growth, right?" He smiled and laughed as he displayed being proud of his accomplishment!

Grace clapped her hands and laughed while Stuart mumbled and shook his head. *A little too much cuteness so early in the morning.*

"Good job, Frank, you are exactly right. And besides we figured a gift card would fit easier in your tool belt rather than the actual shoes! Okay, before you all head out, tell me what you have done so far."

Before the words even left her mouth, everyone enthusiastically shared all the things they had done so far and what lessons they had learned from those things.

Stuart finally spoke as Joshua stood to join the group. He spoke quietly at first, but then a bit louder as he became more comfortable. "I learned a huge lesson last night about fear. I realized how fear is so debilitating that you can really believe someone or something is trying to kill you. When in fact it *is* trying to kill you. It, that is fear, is trying to suck the life right out of you," he held up a clenched fist.

"And it almost won last night." He looked up, "I almost lost the battle. I walk around in a suit all day, pretending to be someone that I'm not just because of fear—fear of

> *Remember—real affirmations, will result in increased productivity and creativity and you'll add to the bottom line. If we focus on the relational part of our business before the bottom line or transactions, we'll see increased business.*

people not liking me because of who I really am on the inside—fear of failure, you name it, I have an issue with fear." No one said anything. Stuart nodded his head, realizing he may have said too much. He looked up and smiled at Joshua.

Joshua asked, "What else?"

Doug held his hand up. "I've got something. "Angela!" He looked in her eyes and said, "Thank you for sharing last night. I could really see a piece of your heart in what you said about your dad. That must have been extremely difficult to lose him like that and to never be able to transition over into womanhood with the approval of your dad. I am so sorry you experienced that."

Angela closed her eyes as a tear ran down her cheek. She pursed her lips and then wiped her eyes with a tissue, avoiding looking in Doug's direction. Everyone was still.

"Thanks, Doug. That was an incredible affirmation," Joshua said, barely above a whisper. Doug nodded.

Angela blew her nose and nodded as well. Then she looked at Doug and mouthed the words, "Thank you."

Abe cleared his throat. "Frank, thanks so much for sharing last night. I am always amazed how many people have stories of some sort of abuse or emotional pain from their past. Your sharing will allow others to open up about their pain as well. I hope you keep sharing. Thanks!"

The group was silent as Frank lowered his head.

After a long time of silence, Joshua finally spoke. "Doug, thank you for sharing last night. Your whole face lit up when you talked about your passion for cooking—am I right folks?" Everyone nodded and clapped.

"Well, since you spoke about that passion, I did some finagling, and today you get to choose what you want to do, head out on the hike with us or hang out in the kitchen with two top chefs and cook dinner tonight."

"Are you serious?" asked Doug. "Oh, I don't think I can do it. I would just hold them up. They don't need a rookie like me messing up their plans."

Angela jumped up and asked, "Are you kidding? This is a perfect opportunity for you. Oh, my gosh, how fun. Doug, you have to do this, unless, of course, you just really want to hike today."

"Well, I really would love to cook with a couple of experienced chefs. And the food has been excellent, so I can only imagine I'll learn some fabulous recipes. Hmm—okay, I would love to stay here and cook for you all."

Angela clapped and reached out to high five Doug. "Yeah, go Doug!"

Joshua said, "And so you shall! I'll give you more information on that in a minute. Anyone else with any thoughts about what we've done so far?"

Everyone was thinking when Joshua spoke again. "Anyone have any questions about anything we've shared so far? Anything that needs further discussion?"

Preston spoke with enthusiasm. "Yeah, yesterday we spent some time on what we are personally responsible for—our own thoughts, our own feelings and our own actions. So I've got that. But then you went on to ask, why do people get so frustrated with others when we are not responsible for what other people do? What is it about how we process what others are saying or doing to us that causes us to get frustrated or upset?"

"Great question, Preston. Anyone want to take a stab at answering?" No one offered an answer.

"Okay," said Joshua. "Well, last night we heard a lot of stories about our backgrounds. Anyway, all the stuff in our past forms who we are today and we're going to talk more about this on our hike this morning. By the way, folks, this is a short day because we have our celebration right up there," he squinted as he looked up on a hillside. "Grab some more food, coffee, or juice and we'll wrap up our breakfast time."

Everyone took their plates to the food table and piled on fresh fruit, freshly baked blueberry scones, a light frittata that slightly bubbled with oozing cheddar, and fresh, strong coffee. The energy and enthusiasm in the air sparked some light chatter and spirited movement.

CHAPTER EIGHTEEN:

Self Identity

Joshua walked up to the head of the table as everyone enjoyed their meal.
"So last night we heard a lot of great stories about memories and folks in our lives that mean something to us. Anyone care to share any thoughts about what you heard or perhaps even thought more about what you shared last night?"

Frank's hand bolted in the air. "I never thought folks would get this deep on a hike. I mean, I sit in a lot of group meetings and trainings and we just don't go this deep." He looked over at Stuart. "I am a little freaked out about what happened last night though."

Stuart ignored him, buried in his own self loathing from having anyone know about his issues with fear.

Frank continued, "I am curious though about something," he raised his eyebrows as he looked at Joshua.

"I know we are on this hike for more than beautiful scenery. Can I ask—what do others think of the story that I shared last night—what do you all think it says about me as a person?"

Joshua sat silently and watched the group.

Angela sat on her hands as she shifted her weight. "Well, Frank, honestly, now I can see why you have the thoughts you believe to be true about yourself—why you would call yourself fearful Frank. You must have lived in fear of your father all those years."

Frank nodded.

Abe looked at Frank, "Frank, I really appreciated you sharing because it takes a lot for a guy to open up like that. I am not so sure I would label you fearful at all. It sounds like the abuse you experienced seared into your soul and is the reason you believe you are fearful. I mean, cowering from your dad—those thoughts you had as a little boy, you believed to be true about yourself based on those experiences."

Frank nodded. "Yep, pretty much!" Frank lifted his chin in the air. "In fact, I remember thinking that the other kids were so much better than me because they were nowhere near as much of a 'scaredy-cat' as I was."

Angela snickered, "Yeah, amazing what we believe to be true about ourselves as we compare ourselves to others."

Linda rested her feet on a chair. "Yep, a bunch of lies is what we end up listening to. And that carries over to our adulthood...I compare myself to other people all the time and I never measure up." She shrugged. "And Lord knows I try to look like the models in magazines. I know better—I will never look like that no matter how hard I try."

Abe joined the conversation and said with enthusiasm, "Every time I go through the line at the grocery store and I see these beautiful women and muscle-bound men on magazine covers and I think, "Geez, I will never look like that guy no matter what I do. But all of our lives we see other people's successes or we compare ourselves to others physically and it affects what we believe to be true about ourselves."

Frank stood and walked to the end of the table, "But what was going on in my mind as a kid was that self-talk stuff. I internalized the thoughts I believed to be true about myself based on what I *believed* others were thinking about me. I thought they all knew I was fearful and so I believed I was indeed fearful."

"Ahhhh," said Joshua as though he were revealing the world's best kept secret. "No one else ever does that, right?"

Many seemed noticeably uncomfortable with the question. Some folded their arms, Preston looked away and Doug leaned back in his chair, moving a toothpick up and down in his mouth.

"What's the key word Frank said?

Only Angela responded, "Believe!"

"What's that mean?" asked Abe.

"I make things up in my head. I think I know the perceptions other people have of me," commented Doug as he tilted his head to one side.

Joshua was silent as he watched Doug process the question he just asked.

Doug nodded slowly. "Actually, I do make up conclusions in my head. And I can grow very confident about what other people think of me. How weird?"

"Actually, Doug, it really is quite normal. We all do it. We all have this talking stuff going on in our heads, remember we talked about this already." Joshua used his right hand to form a hand puppet by his right ear, "Those voices just talk and talk and talk. . . .

"Look," Joshua continued, "let's think about this, how often do you think your thoughts about yourself or your self-identity is impacted by first impressions and your hippocampus by how things are communicated?"

Frank said, "All the time. Geez, we're messed up!" Everyone chuckled.

"Nah," Grace smiled. "You're just becoming aware. And once you know any new truth, the question then becomes a matter of deciding what are you going to do about it?"

"Change it," everyone responded.

"Good," said Grace. Preston sat up straight.

"Preston? You look like you might be pondering something," Grace said.

"I think I am," Preston said. "I just never thought about 'the thoughts I believe to be true about myself' and what all that means. I mean, this makes sense as we look at Frank's life. I'll have to think about how to apply this to my life, how I grew up, etc."

"Thanks, Preston," Joshua said softy. "Remember, the type of change we're talking about here is a process, not an event. It is more along the lines of a metamorphosis, similar to a butterfly's. It takes time. Remember the hippocampus? We have a number of events stored in our minds? An event happened that had passion or emotion, and purpose, it goes through the hippocampus, and is parked in our long-term memories. These events affect our long-term memories. And these memories attribute to our self-identity.

"The only way our self-identity can change is if we surround ourselves with people who are truthful, what we call "bumper people," which we'll explain later, right?"

"How would you like to have a positive self-identity? Are you willing to get into relationships with people who will be truthful with you? People who love you enough to share the truth with you and—can you hear the truth?"

> ### *Self Identity and How It's Formed:*
>
> *The thoughts I believe to be true about myself*
>
> 1. Personal Experiences: *The thoughts I believe to be true about myself as a result of life's experiences.*
> 2. Social Comparisons: *The thoughts I think about myself as I compare myself to others.*
> 3. Internalizing Others Judgment: *The thoughts I believe to be true about myself based on what I believe what others are thinking of me.*

Stuart let out a short laugh, and then quickly apologized when he realized no one else laughed. "Sorry, I couldn't help but think about the movie *A Few Good Men* when Nicholson shouts, 'You can't handle the truth!'" Stuart did his best imitation of the actor.

Joshua smiled as he looked at Stuart and said, "Great movie! As dramatic as that scene was, it *was* the truth. Many people cannot handle the truth!"

Frank coughed and said, "Stuart, I need to apologize to you." Frank looked directly at Stuart who lowered his head.

"Last night when you needed me, I bolted out of the cabin when I should have stuck around to help you. I knew there was nothing in the cabin but as soon as I heard you yell, I was gone. I guess in my hippocampus is a memory about being dreadfully scared in close quarters—if I could get out of my house, I was safe because I knew my dad wouldn't come after me with the neighbors watching. So I am sorry I didn't help you."

Stuart lifted his head to look at Frank and their eyes met. *Someone else who really does understand fear!*

"I'm sorry, will you forgive me?"

Stuart nodded his head, "Of course I do. Thanks."

"Will—"

Stuart jumped up from the table, not wanting to hear anymore of the uncomfortable interchange. "We're good, Frank, thanks!" He walked to the food table and scooped a heaping of fruit on his plate.

But Frank stood and walked over to Stuart. "Stuart, I want you to have this." He handed him his card that had his intro speech. "I hope we can get to know one another better through life together!!"

Stuart gave an exasperated look but then took the card and shook Frank's hand.

As everyone finished their breakfast, Grace said, "Time for you all to head out because I don't know about you all but I want you to get this part of the hike done so we can celebrate tonight! But first I have a present!!"

She handed everyone a beautiful gold plated key that had inscribed, "Self Identity."

As she watched everyone hold their key and oohhh and awww, she said, "Now you are fitting the pieces of the puzzle together."

Everyone nodded as they looked at Grace and acknowledged they understood.

Everyone waved to Grace as they gathered their things. "Have a great time and see you soon!" Frank gave her a hug goodbye as did Angela.

Joshua clapped his hands in applause, so everyone followed. "Okay, then let's hit the trail. Just because it's a short day doesn't mean we don't have a lot of ground to cover," he winked. "Oh, wait." He took a piece of paper from his pocket and handed it to Doug. "The chef's are expecting you any minute. Head down that slope over there to a set of steps. You'll see them. Alphonso will meet up with you there," and he pointed over the hillside. "Have a blast!"

Doug grabbed his stuff. "Guess I'll take this back to the cabin," he looked excitedly at everyone. "I'll see you all in time for dinner. Be prepared for a treat," he said confidently.

"Have fun!" everyone shouted.

Joshua took his stick and pounded it. By now the team knew this was the signal to walk.

Frank spoke. "What if you have a lot of fear from your hippocampus? How do you handle it?"

"Great question, Frank. It's important to remember that what you are learning on this hike is just part of a process. Many things stem from what we know or have experienced and are now stored in our long-term memory. It is different for everyone," he stopped and looked Frank in the eye. "The fact that you are asking questions, admitting your fear, and being willing to talk about it openly is a huge step, Frank, good job! Excellent, in fact." Frank beamed as Joshua spoke.

"Many of us deal with fear or other issues that are so deep we don't even know it. When we do begin to recognize those constraints it is important to be open to acknowledge they are there, why they exist, and ways to deal with them. That is just the beginning of the healing process. Personally," Joshua smiled at Frank, "my healing has come through my faith. I'm not really sure it can come any other way." Joshua stood in silence as he looked at each person.

"Okay," he clapped his hands startling everyone. "Let's go! Anyone want to learn a bit more about leadership today? Do you think everything we've done so far has set the foundation to learn and understand how to remove our personal constraints that keep us from being good leaders?"

"Absolutely!"

While the others prepared to move out Joshua said to Linda, "You lead the way again today."

"Joshua, I really am in no mood to lead. I have no idea where I'm going."

"That's interesting, Linda, because you've made it clear to us that you are a natural born leader."

"I never said any such thing. People just naturally put me in charge."

"Oh, so you're saying you don't take charge, people put you in charge, correct?"

"Yep, and I can't help that."

"Okay, then, that's exactly what I'm doing. I am putting you in charge of leading. How's that? Now let's walk. Linda, lead the way, please. We're going that way," Joshua pointed to his right.

They started out close together, but as time went on they formed a single line, one behind the other.

They walked for two hours in almost complete silence, each one pondering a different thought, watching their steps and looking up only long enough to make sure they were following the right path.

Stuart ran to eventually catch up to Joshua. With short bursts of breath he asked Joshua, "Do you really believe all this stuff that you teach or is it just a leadership course you thought might make a great hike even more interesting?"

"It is the core of my being. I absolutely, unequivocally believe it. But you bring up a good point, Stuart. What do you believe core beliefs are?"

"Something you believe in right down to your very core, I guess, I'm not really sure."

"Well, psychiatrists say a core belief is a belief you hold so true and so much a part of you that you cannot change it. Some say a core belief is something we would go to death to defend.

"So, do you believe a core belief can get in your way? And can a good positive core belief be a constraint?" Joshua pounded the path with his stick.

"Yeah, I think a core belief can get in our way. Especially if it is some religious belief or some sort of political belief that keeps us from seeing what really is right or correct."

"Hmm, interesting point. Do you believe core beliefs can change?"

Stuart shrugged, "Don't know. Guess not if they are truly what psychiatrists say they are."

"Well, this is my thought and just my opinion. I believe they *can* change. When we take our core beliefs and place them on other people and expect them to agree, we place a constraint on our relationship—an unfair constraint, mind you."

Stuart looked at Joshua, "I can see that! But what's that got to do with everything we've been talking about?"

Both men stopped walking as Joshua pulled out a towel, and wiped the sweat off his forehead. "Stuart," he looked him right in the eye, "in the core of your being, do you believe you are a leader?"

Stuart said, "No, Joshua, I don't, because, in the depths of my heart, I don't believe anyone would want to follow me." He turned and started walking again.

CHAPTER NINETEEN:

Leadership

"Hold up, guys, we're going to break for an early lunch" shouted Joshua. "Let's head over to this clearing." Linda, who was leading the group, fell behind everyone as they made a turn to follow Joshua. Preston and Angela were having a lively conversation.

Everyone dove in and piled their plates with fresh vegetables, steaming grilled chicken, hummus, pasta salad, olives and warm pita bread rubbed lightly with olive oil. Joshua popped an olive into his mouth and chewed, waiting to swallow before saying, "So, do you all mind if I do a little teaching here?"

"No, said Frank with his mouth full. "We love it when you teach—at least I do!" He looked at the others sheepishly. The others nodded as well.

"Great. Well, we've been talking about leadership..."

"We have?" asked Linda. "I don't feel like we've even remotely talked about anything pertaining to leadership."

"Au contraire, Linda," said Joshua. "*Everything* we've talked about has to do with leadership: how we communicate, how we relate, breaking through constraints. You name it, it's about leadership. I know, sounds a bit crazy, doesn't it, but admittedly—it is transforming!"

"Boy, you can say that again," said Angela as she broke a piece of bread and dipped it into the hummus on her plate.

"So, let me ask you all, what exactly is the definition of leadership? Or, at least, what I would call 'appropriate' leadership?"

Everyone spoke at once, stepping over each other's words.

Preston puffed out his chest and said, "Clearly, when you have a position of power, you are a leader."

"Leadership is when you influence others to do something, reach a goal or change a process—something like that!" said Linda.

"Well, let's think about this. If you Google the word 'leadership' you will get almost a million results. A million results, folks! No wonder we don't know what leadership is. Now I am not saying Google is the place we should go to find the answers, but it does prove a point. Do you believe we have a crisis going on in our world because no one knows what appropriate leadership is? And, admittedly, in today's world we have very few examples of good leadership.

"I believe," Joshua continued, "leadership is when one is willing to lay down his or her life for those they lead or with whom they have influence. Just think about it for a moment. When one is willing to lay down his or her life for those they lead or with whom they have influence!

"The key word here is 'LIFE.' That can mean many things: tell me what you think 'life' means?

"My stuff."

"My own agenda."

"My pride?"

"Great answers." Joshua walked over to a small stream running alongside the path. In the middle of the stream was a fairly good-sized rock. "Here's an example. This rock represents *my* life. It certainly serves a purpose but right now, what is it doing?"

"Getting in the way of the natural flow of the water," said Frank.

"Yep." Joshua leaned down and with two hands picked up the rock and effortlessly moved it to the side of the stream. "What just happened?"

Frank responded enthusiastically, "You got the heck out of the way, Joshua!" he chuckled.

"Even more important than that, Frank. I got me and my agenda out of the way! And then what happened?"

"The stream became free to move and flow at a quicker pace!" said Angela.

"Good. I literally set aside my own life and my own personal agenda, which is a constraint," he said as he pointed to the rock. "And guess what happens?" He pointed to the area where the rock had been sitting. My serving others then makes their lives free to flow. They are more

> **Definition of Leadership:**
> *When one is willing to lay down his or her life for those they lead or with whom they have influence.*

productive, more creative, and are no longer bound up." Joshua knocked his fists together and held them as if invisible handcuffs were around his wrists. "And when you give your life to serve others, those you lead and others—watch out!" Joshua's fists opened as he lifted his hands up in the air, looked to the sky, and let out a light-hearted laugh. "Talk about things flowing and freedom and creativity! Wow!" His joy lit the faces of everyone around him as they smiled and laughed as well.

He shook his head and let out a breath. "Tons of leadership books will tell you to be a good leader and that you have to serve others. The best way to do that is to love God first. "

Silence.

Joshua's face was solemn as he nodded and took in a deep breath. The sounds of birds chirping and squirrels scampering through the trees were the only sounds anyone could hear. Joshua spoke softly, as he held his hands up and cupped his eyes. "We have our eyes so focused on our stuff and our world and our things that we lose sight of all that is important to us, including God. Then we go to do an outreach over here," he moved his hands in a circular motion to the side, "and we call that serving others and we mark it off our task list and we go back to our stuff." Again he cupped his eyes. "I want us to see not only way beyond the box, but way beyond ourselves." He stretched his long arms high above his head.

"So, any questions, anyone," he asked as a smile returned to his face.

Preston raised his hand, "I hate to always be the one who questions things, Joshua."

"It's okay, Preston!" encouraged Joshua.

"Well, what if your own life—or desire—*is* to love and serve God and others? Why would you have to lay it down or set it aside?"

Joshua waited a moment as he watched Preston, but didn't say a word as a smile slowly crossed his face.

Preston, in turn, watched Joshua, and, as the smile on Joshua's face broadened, he started nodding. "Oh," said Preston as his eyes lit up. "I get it! When you really are living that out, THAT'S when you are truly a leader. Am I right? Am I?" Preston surprisingly almost giggled.

Joshua leaned his head back and laughed. "Geez, you guys are good at answering your own questions." He gave Preston a high five. "How 'bout we change your name from Prideful Preston to Perceptive Preston?"

Preston put his finger to his chin and nodded. "I like that!"

"Great, so from now on we will call Preston, Perceptive Preston because you truly are wise," said Joshua on a serious note as he looked into Preston's eyes. "Use the wisdom for good," he said as he turned to address the rest of the group.

Stuart watched, as the two exchanged looks that made Stuart wonder how on earth Joshua does what he does. How does he change someone's attitude from steeping in pride to showing real wisdom and then sharing it with others? *How does he do that?*

Stuart watched everyone fall into line behind Joshua as he led the group on the trail again. The struggle ensued within Stuart to not give in to the dark voice. He could not shake the feeling that the path Joshua was on was the right path and he wanted more of it. But then he struggled with not wanting to be perceived as weak. He leaned down to the stream and splashed water on his face and shook his head. *Don't give in to the dark voice— let it go.* He jumped up and followed behind the others.

CHAPTER TWENTY:

V-STTEELE and Lead

As they continued to walk, Joshua said, "Now, we've talked about the **definition** of leadership, which is . . ."

"When one is willing to lay down his or her life for those they lead or with whom they have influence."

"Great! Now we're going to learn the **purpose** of leadership. I am going to open your eyes and your mind to some things that you may not be aware of regarding leadership." Joshua stopped, turning around to face the team. "Stop where you are. Just be still. Be really still for a moment." A comfortable silence was in the air and they drank in the stillness of the rich forest for several minutes.

"Now," Joshua whispered almost magically, "tell me what you see."

Everyone looked around and shrugged their shoulders except Angela. She stepped forward, and, with a sweeping motion of her hands, she began painting a picture. "I see a beautiful, long archway of trees that looks like a row of large Roman soldiers. The trees look like they are leaning over toward one another, stretching over the open pathway with crossed arms as if to provide a protective shield for anyone who walks under them."

"Wow, that was great, Angela." Joshua turned and looked behind him to see the beautiful picture Angela painted. "I see it!" Everyone clapped in agreement. Angela blushed and made a slight curtsy.

"Hmmm," Joshua said as he narrowed his eyes and looked at Angela. "Now, what was your name again?"

Angela didn't answer him as the blush in her cheeks deepened and she lowered her head.

Joshua tapped his chin with his forefinger. "I believe it was Angry Angela or something like that?"

Angela looked up and locked eyes with Joshua as he said, "I believe we should call you Articulate Angela, because that was very well stated!"

A smile slowly rolled across Angela's face as she began to beam. "I like that Joshua. Thank you so much."

"And you are welcome! Okay. Does everyone see the same thing now?" Everyone looked beyond Joshua and nodded as they saw the picture Angela described unfold before their eyes.

"Great, here's what I want us to do. Get into a single line behind me. Abe, would you go to the back of the line? Now everyone place your right hand on the shoulder of the person in front of you, just your right hand."

Everyone followed directions. Frank had his hand on Joshua's shoulder, Linda put hers on Frank's shoulder, Angela placed hers on Linda's, Preston's on Angela, Stuart put his hand on Preston's shoulder and then Abe put his big hand on Stuart's shoulder.

"Great! Now close your eyes and walk straight ahead. The person in front of you will lead you. Start with your right foot."

As they took a few steps they were amazed that they did not trip all over each other. They walked for several feet, laughing and talking, curious about what they might discover.

"Now, in a few yards we're going to stop. And when we do, I want you to keep your eyes closed. Everyone understand that?"

"Yep."

"Get ready—okay—stop and keep your eyes closed."

Everyone stopped right where they were.

"Keep your eyes closed." Joshua led each team member forward a few steps to stand right next to one another, shoulder to shoulder. "Now, everyone, open your eyes."

They all opened their eyes and collectively gasped. They dared not take a step because they stood on a large cement block right on the edge of a very tall cliff that looked out over an expanse of mountains, valleys, forests, and buildings that from their view looked like monopoly game pieces. Before them was a railing firmly rooted in the cement block. Preston walked up to it to get a closer look.

"Wow!" Preston said as he took hold of the railing. "Oh my gosh. This is beautiful!"

"Well, you should be quite familiar with this whole area," said Joshua as he swept his hand in the air across the great expanse of the wooded area. "This is where we've been walking the past few days. Over there is where we started, and over there," he turned to the right, "is our camping area. That is where we were day one. Almost right below us is where we were on day two."

"How on earth did we get all the way up here today, in the short amount of time we've been walking?" asked Preston.

Joshua looked at Preston and patted him on the shoulder. "It's a process, not a one-time event, my friend." He looked at the team and said, "See, you all had no idea that this is where you had been walking. You were so busy watching out for stones and rocks and tree limbs and wondering where lunch came from," he winked at Stuart, "that you missed the big picture. Actually, from where you were walking, you couldn't even see the big picture. At least not until I brought you to this point.

"There is truth in the saying, 'you can't see the forest for the trees.' However, as your leader, it was up to me to cast the vision of the bigger picture for you. I needed to bring you to a place where I could cast the vision. How many of you believe you could have come to this point, looked out at this beautiful landscape and known this is where you had been walking all this time? You needed a leader to cast the vision and point out the various landmarks, right?"

Stuart, who had been unusually quiet, nodded, "Yeah, no way would I have ever figured that out—I don't know about anyone else. But I am really just trying to piece together what this has to do with the purpose of leadership."

"Great, Stuart, thanks! You've raised an excellent question. What does this have to do with leadership? Well, as your leader, I led you to this point; I cast the vision for the bigger picture and helped you see that bigger, broader picture. It is not enough to just cast the vision. You must help people 'see' the vision as well. Draw them into the vision as best you can."

"So, what you're saying," said Preston, "is that we should take Angela to every vision casting meeting with us so she can paint the picture?"

Angela smacked Preston's arm which produced several chuckles.

"Let me ask you this. Would you have guessed that this beautiful area lay right beyond the archway of trees back there?"

"No," said a couple as they shook their heads.

"What if I would have just told you it was there, but continued walking through the forest?"

"I would have never been able to really experience what I am seeing by you just telling me," said Frank.

"Exactly, Frank, thank you. By drawing the folks you lead into the vision, you are no longer simply telling them or even teaching them about it, you are..."

"Involving them," said Angela.

"And what happens when you involve them?"

"They understand!"

"Excellent! Now check this out." Joshua pulled a notebook from his backpack and started drawing. He turned the pad around and showed everyone a simple sketch.

"What do you see?"

"A triangle." Preston said first. "But I know you by now, Joshua. It can't be just a triangle. It has to be more than that, right?"

"Yep, so think of this as it relates to leadership." Several cocked their heads to the side and peered closer.

Stuart jumped in and responded, "It's an org chart."

"A what chart?" asked Frank.

"An org chart," he repeated as he moved closer to Joshua. He pointed to the triangle, "At the top here you have the leader, or CEO, and then all his minions are under him."

"Well," smiled Joshua, "you have the org chart piece correct. This is a typical organizational chart with the leader at the top. Now, I want you to 'change the thought' here a bit. Rather than thinking the leader is at the top and the rest are beneath the leader, I want you to think of the leader here," he pointed to the pinnacle of the triangle, "and that the leader is casting a vision." Joshua drew on the pad of paper once again.

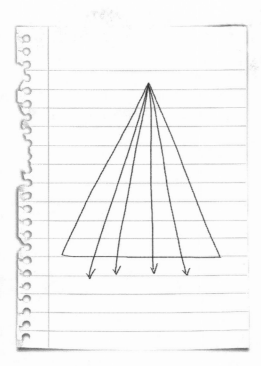

"The position of the leader in this form of organizational chart is merely to cast vision. Now, interestingly enough, some people call this command and control. This is where the leader is at the top and barking orders to everyone below. Not good! The leader should be in this position to **cast vision**." He looked back over the view where the group was standing and he opened his arms outward in a V shape. "This model is very important, because the leader must cast a vision and involve the others in seeing that vision." He looked out of the side of his eye at the team. "Are you seeing what I am seeing?"

Everyone nodded slowly, taking in every word Joshua spoke.

"This, folks, is the WHY of what leaders do. Cast the Vision—WHY do we exist or our organizations exist? Where are we going and what is unique about who we are and what we do? It is imperative we be very clear in communicating that vision so that others see it and understand."

Then he pointed to their immediate right where a gently flowing, clear stream bubbled easily over the rocks. The sun glistened on the water and bounced off in various directions, giving the water a playful flow.

"What do you see?"

"A stream?" everyone answered cautiously, knowing there was more to the question.

Sensing their hesitation, Joshua said enthusiastically, "Excellent! Yes! A stream . . . *and* it is not just any stream! Come with me."

And with that he turned, stepped off the cement block they were standing on, and walked a few feet along the ledge of the cliff. He cautiously turned to descend a flight of man-made steps with rails on the left side. The steps were just wide enough for one person, so the team followed in single file, trusting Joshua's every move.

Stuart lingered behind, debating within himself the possibility of quickly throwing himself over the cliff. *This could be the place. No one would ever suspect—it would look so natural.* Abe came up from behind and placed his hand on his shoulder. "You okay, buddy?"

"Yeah, yeah, I'm good," said Stuart as he continued to follow the rest of the team. *There has to be a place. Just keep your eyes peeled and don't think about it anymore. Just do it.*

The steps twisted and turned in every direction before they came to a landing. They walked under a trestle full of bursting red and pink roses and other brightly colored flowers. This was only the opening to the beautiful scene that unfolded before them. Just beyond the final archway was a beautiful meadow of wildflower blossoms. Many of the blooms were so large they resembled bushes that had been spray painted with the boldest colors. The grassy knoll was thick like a rich green carpet that beckoned the observer to take the challenge to kick off their shoes and run through barefoot. On the right side was a rugged, craggy hillside with flowers popping through the rocks and stretching their colorful blossoms upward toward the sun, drinking in every ray of light. So vivid were the colors that it almost seemed like new colors were being created with the passing of clouds overhead.

Out on the hillside, a gentle stream flowed and gained momentum as it cascaded over the rocks and landed into a pool of water below.

"Wow!" was all the team could say.

"That's the stream we saw up on the ridge, isn't it?" asked Angela.

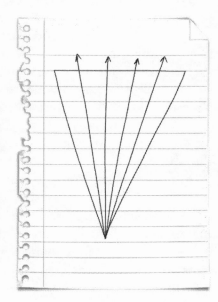

Joshua nodded and struck the ground with his walking stick, signaling the team to follow. He walked over to the water and stooped down. He cupped his hand and splashed water into his face. Then he shook his head and Preston and Abe did the same. Then Frank, Stuart and Angela followed.

"Hmmm," said Angela. "This is so clear and beautiful and deliciously refreshing!" Linda stood back with her arms folded. "Don't want to ruin my make-up!"

Joshua continued. "Angela, you were right-on in discovering the waterfall. It is in fact the stream we saw above from the cliff. That tiny stream, as it dropped down over the side of the mountain, gained so much momentum and became the falls that we see here." He pointed to the top of the mountain. "And that tiny stream of water up above that pours itself into this pool of water serves this entire meadow, making the flowers so incredibly vibrant, yes?" Everyone held their gaze; smiling as they looked at the area as Joshua gestured and waved his hand over the area.

Joshua pulled the notepad out of his backpack and once again began drawing. He turned the pad around for everyone to see.

"Okay, tell me once again, what do you see?"

"Uh, an upside down pyramid?" asked Stuart.

"Yes," shouted Joshua. "This is typically what everyone describes as the servant leader organizational model. And that's true. The leader is at the bottom and serves the people. I think it is important that the leader 'serve' the vision that's been cast, but even more than that! This is where I believe leaders not only serve, but they teach, train, and equip their people. This is crucial to an organization being successful. It is not enough to cast a vision," he pointed to the right side up pyramid. "A leader must also be willing to serve, then teach, then train, then equip."

"What's the difference between teach and train?" asked Frank.

"Great question, Frank. Anyone want to answer him?"

"I'll take a stab," said Stuart. "I think when you teach, you are just giving information, basically instructing someone on what to do. When you train, you are 'showing' them what a good job looks like, you're demonstrating the job for them."

"Like 'tell me, I forget; teach me, I remember; and involve me, I understand'. Training is the 'involve me' part," said Angela.

Joshua remained silent and hushed the group. From behind a shaggy bush, only yards away, a doe peered out to investigate this human interference. She cautioned to her fawn to stay close. The doe jumped over a flowering bush but her baby stopped just short of the bush. The fawn then turned to scamper back the way she had come. Mama deer jumped back over the bush and circled around the baby, gently nudging her to jump. After a minute or two, the doe leaped over the bush, and this time the baby imitated and followed directions exactly. And off they ran together, kicking up their heels, and raced through the flowering meadow.

"Did you see that?" asked Joshua as his eyes widened. "I have seen this over and over again. I never, ever get tired of seeing the miracle of a mama doe and her baby. But this was so much more.

Joshua turned back to Angela. "Angela, you are exactly right!" laughed Joshua. "And the deer interaction was perfect timing! The mama had been teaching the baby how to jump for some time now. You may not know this about deer, but when they have a baby, they leave it in a safe place with lots of brush and a place to hide in. Then the mama goes to find food for herself so she can nurse the baby. But the mama stays within 500 yards or so of the fawn. She had to jump over bushes and other things to get in and out of the safe haven where the baby was and the baby watched the mama the whole time. So the baby was being *taught* how to jump. Today, you saw the mama *train* the baby to jump and the baby followed and was successful.

"This is where most leadership courses fall short. They teach you mostly how to do just the WHAT of leadership which is very important, but there's the 'Missing Link.' We believe when a leader serves, teaches, trains, and equips, they need to do a great job in serving first. Then provide the WHAT which is teaching and providing information about the task. Then leaders need to provide the HOW which is training and show HOW to do the task. And finally when leaders equip, they provide the tools needed to do the task, the strategy. Equipping provides the details of WHEN, WHERE, WHO—are you following me?"

"We think so."

"Let's keep processing because it will become clearer. Now, come with me alongside the path here," said Joshua as he slowly made his way around the edge of the water. "Now lean in a bit closer, right where the falls hits the water. What do you see?"

Everyone leaned closer to the place where Joshua pointed and peered into the water.

"You're looking too closely," said Joshua. So they backed away, their faces skewed with uncertainty.

"Hmm," said Abe. "I think I remember this part—not sure I understood it the first go around."

"Well, tell us Abe!" said Angela.

Abe looked at Joshua, who nodded an approval.

"Well, I see bubbles."

"Bubbles?" repeated everyone in disbelief.

"Yep, bubbles."

"Well, duh, Abe, we all see bubbles forming, but that's not what he's looking for. He's looking for something profound, like a sideways triangle or something," said Preston. "Everyone, keep looking."

"A sideways triangle?" asked Frank quietly under his breath. "How can a triangle be sideways?"

Abe tried to hold back a laugh. "Well, you see the bubbles. Do you remember what forms a bubble?"

Frank said, "Well in this particular instance, it's the agitated mixture of water and air. When the pressure on the outside is the same as the pressure on the inside, it forms a perfect sphere of liquid or gas—a bubble. And," he continued, "we want to keep moving and being flexible even if it means moving through a painful change. And that may even mean bursting, or laying down my life, and making an abundance of other bubbles!"

Everyone stared at Frank as Abe nodded and Joshua clapped.

Joshua said, "Thanks, Frank. Wow! Good job! Perhaps we should change your name from Fretful to flexible or better yet, to Fearless. Yeah, Fearless Frank."

Frank nodded and smiled.

Joshua then turned his attention to his writing pad and began furiously drawing.

"So tell me, what do you see?"

"An atom?" answered Linda

"Almost."

"Uh, bubbles?" asked Stuart

"Yep, bubbles. This, my friends, is your third organizational chart. Your 'think way beyond the bubble' chart! Each one of these bubbles represents the first organization chart, remember cast vision, as well as organizational chart two, which is to serve, teach, train, and equip. A good leader continually moves through all three charts. All three are important.

"But this one," he said as he pointed to the bubble chart, "this

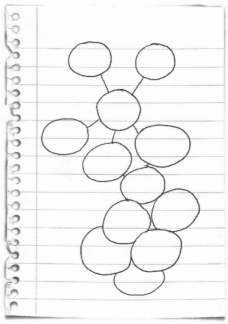

is where true empowerment and productivity lie. This is where organizational cultures change, where transformation begins and where leaders truly move from transaction to relationship. This is where they empower, then let go and as important, evaluate. After empowering, a truly effective leader will let go of control and check in every so often to encourage, affirm and give counsel if needed as they continually serve, teach, train and equip." Joshua had a look in his eye that Stuart had not seen before. Stuart knew the information Joshua shared ignited the fire and passion in him.

Joshua continued. "See the lines between the bubbles? The lines represent relationships—strong, healthy, whole relationships." He reached over and scooped up a handful of bubbles. "And the stronger and healthier the relationships become, the less you will see lines between the bubbles."

He blew the bubbles in the air. "And, as Frank said, when the pressure becomes too much, on the outside or inside, the bubbles burst and become smaller and more abundant."

Everyone seemed to understand these ideas.

Purpose of Leadership:
Cast Vision
Serve
Teach
Train
Equip
Empower
Let Go
Evaluate

"And," Joshua continued, "you cannot skip from the first chart right to the 'bubble' chart. You must go from the first chart, then the second chart, then the bubble chart, and then back to the first chart, and eventually, over time, you will operate in the purely functional bubble chart. Then you're always casting vision, serving, teaching, training, and equipping. At this point," he pointed to the bubble chart, "you as a leader can empower others and 'let go' and periodically check in to evaluate how things are going.

"Folks, this model is the difference between 'being' and 'doing.' It is the difference between relational and transactional. Everybody understand?"

"Amazingly, yes," said an astounded Stuart!

"So, let me ask a question. Which came first, the form of the bubble or the function of the bubble?"

Suddenly, the group was very confused.

"Which came first," Joshua repeated slowly, "the form of the bubble or the function?"

"Oh, I get it," Stuart jumped in, suddenly reinvigorated because of the challenge put before him. "The answer is form. The form of the bubble came first so it can perform its function as a bubble!" Stuart said proudly.

"Ahhh, great attempt, but not so fast, Sherlock! Think about this. The agitated water—where did it come from?

"The water fall."

"Great, and then it mixed with what?

"Air."

"Good, so the coming together of the air and the agitated water is the what?

"Function?" asked Stuart.

"Yes! And, because of that function, what happened?"

"The form of the bubble emerged!"

"So, this is where most companies get into trouble. Function always comes before formation or, function before position. See, we jump into setting up a system, we have the organizational chart set, and then we have all the blocks set on that organizational chart. Then we decide to put a specific function into that form. And guess what? It's not working folks!" Joshua was animated.

"Decide what functions you need in order to run your organization. Hear me, I said functions. I did not say positions. Don't decide you want a VP of marketing and then decide what you need that person to do. Decide the function you need and then decide how the various functions will work together. See, we have been taught form comes first. So let's undo that thinking.

"Not only that," Joshua continued, "most organizations believe when they want to make a cultural change, they begin with the entire organization. They cannot make a change at that level unless the leader has done what?"

"Cast vision," said Abe.

"Serve?" asked Stuart.

"Teach," said Frank

"Train," said Linda.

"Equip," said Angela

"Empower," said Preston.

"Excellent!" said Joshua. "And a leader must do them in order. You cannot go from serve to empower. Ever wonder why organizations are in trouble today? Because leaders go from teaching to empowering, thinking they are doing their team a favor. Wrong! That is the biggest disservice you can do for a team. You have to go in this order: Cast the vision, serve, teach, train, equip, empower. And once you empower your team, then what?"

"You can let go and evaluate," said Angela.

"Good job. And we've given this model a name. It's **V-STTEELE and Lead**. You cast vision, serve, teach, train, equip, empower, let go and evaluate. Make sense?"

Everyone nodded.

Joshua took in a deep breath and let it out. "A nugget of wisdom for you folks...when a leader follows this process all the questions get answered in the way most folks are wired—WHY, WHAT, HOW, WHEN, WHERE, WHO. The relationships among team members will be healthier and stronger.

"Your team will be more creative and productive and a great by-product of all that is. . .?"

"They have more fun!" shouted Doug.

"Exactly right, Doug." Joshua stood for a moment as he studied the faces of everyone. He then nodded and pounded his stick and everyone followed him.

They walked to the other side of the meadow. Joshua looked as though he were headed right for the mountain when he ducked inside a cave. Everyone stooped down and walked into a lighted cavern and moved slowly. They came to an opening that led outside to a platform. Parked by the side of the mountain was a cable car, opened and waiting.

Joshua stood next to the door and waved his hand. "Ladies and gentlemen, please step into the car." Everyone took a spot in the car and held a strap that was suspended from the ceiling.

Stuart took in a deep breath. All the teachings Joshua and Abe offered over the last couple of days started to swirl in his head, but instead of causing confusion, they aligned with a sense in his soul.

With a jolt, the car moved off the platform and into the open air, suspended only by a cable. "Hold on," laughed Joshua, "because we're heading higher up and digging in a little deeper."

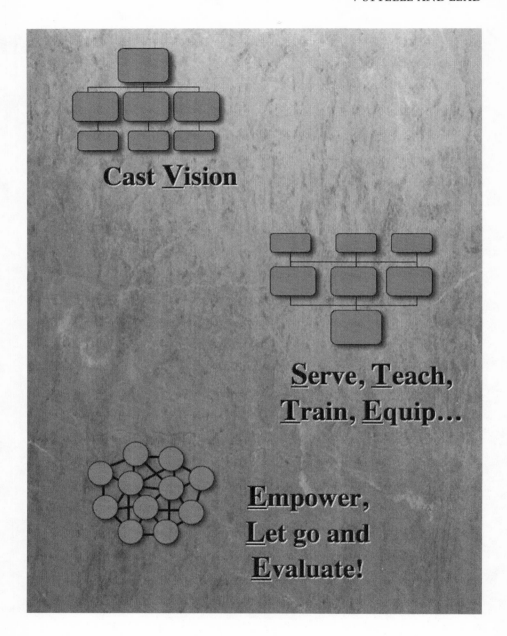

Cast **V**ision

Serve, **T**each,
Train, **E**quip…

Empower,
Let go and
Evaluate!

THE FUNCTIONAL MODEL: WHY, WHAT, HOW,

WHEN, WHERE, AND WHO.

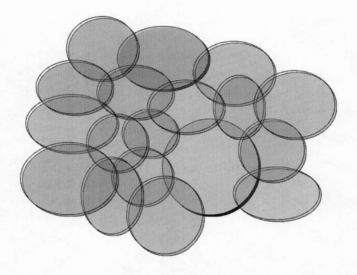

We must continually move through all three models before

we can solely operate in the Functional Model only.

CHAPTER TWENTY ONE:

Laying Down Your Life

The cable car shifted into gear and headed up the hillside. At times they drifted right above the hillside and other times they lifted higher over meadows. The car came to a stop and within minutes they were standing at the top of a mountain, at a higher altitude than they had been the whole hike. They stood for a moment as they breathed in the fresh air and looked out over the beautiful mountainside.

"Welcome, my friends!"

Everyone turned around, and there stood Doug, wearing a food-stained chef tunic and a smile a mile long, his arms wide open and welcoming. Grace stood right next to him, smiling as well.

After the jubilant greetings, the team sat down to eat. It was turning dusk and a beautiful blanket of stars emerged overhead. The gentle breeze cast a savory aroma around them.

Doug shared all that he had experienced that day. As he spoke with animation and enthusiasm, exuding confidence, Stuart watched intently. "I want that!" He whispered to himself. "I want whatever Doug seems to have."

It's not too late, he heard another voice, the same voice he'd squelched for many years.

Doug stood at the head of the table and pointed to various dishes, explaining each one in detail. The team enjoyed Doug's delicious meal, and Stuart for the first time saw a tiny droplet of hope that rippled through his sea of despair. He witnessed Doug doing what he loved—and not a trace of doubt was evident from Doug. He was totally transformed and he came alive. Stuart saw a chance to move from the dark voice into a place of freedom . . . fragmented glimpses of hope like rays of sunshine peeking through the dark, ominous clouds, ever so faint but evident none the less.

Stuart sat up straight as he listened intently to the group continue to affirm Doug and one another. As they finished the meal and spent a few moments relaxing, Stuart wandered off by himself to think a bit and to drink in the beautiful scenery, pondering all he had heard and learned.

Just then, *crack*—the sound of a breaking twig startled him. He held his breath and hesitated to turn around, afraid of what he might see. It was Linda.

"Thought I'd come see what's so interesting over here," she said in a sultry voice which stirred something in Stuart. He could not put his finger on it but he had a desire of some sort. *This could be interesting*, he thought to himself!

She looked out over the mountain and clutched her arms to warm herself, "This truly is gorgeous!"

Stuart took a cautious step around to look at the same view. Just then he lost his footing. His arms flailed up and down frantically—"Oh my God, help—help me!" he yelled as the rocks under his feet gave way and he tumbled down a slope. Desperately trying to regain his footing, he continued to slide down the mountain, destined to plummet into the vast rocky valley below.

He gasped as he reached for something, anything to hold onto. Clawing wildly, he finally grabbed a ledge in the rock. He hung suspended in air, with rocks continuing to fall past him.

With fear in his eyes, he looked at Linda, who held her hands over her mouth, wide eyed. Stuart mouthed the words, 'help me.' He let out a scream and almost lost his grip, the rocks sliding beneath his hands.

Breathless—*my God, wh—what—help me! Help--H!* Just then he heard another voice, a panicky voice—*Go ahead, let go. It's perfect, can't you see? This is just what you wanted, this is your chance!*

Linda tried to scream but the words wouldn't come. She looked back where the group had gathered and finally let out a scream, desperate for someone to hear them and come to their aid.

"Help—please help me." His breaths were as jagged as the rocks that were cutting into the pads of his fingertips. "I—I, I can't hold on much longer."

Linda's face was frozen in fear. Stuart closed his eyes and took in a deep breath ready to let go rather than face his fears and ask God for strength. But then something took over and he looked down and cried, "God, please help me. I don't want to die—please!!"

Suddenly, Abe's face appeared looking over the cliff as he reached out his hand. "Come on buddy. Grab my hand."

Stuart slowly shook his head no, with resignation in his eyes. But Abe was not ready to give up. He reached his arm further over the edge while Joshua stood behind him, holding on to Abe. They both screamed, "REACH!"

"I can't," said Stuart barely above a whisper as his left arm began to let go.

Abe screamed, "Stuart, REACH!"

Stuart closed his eyes and took in a deep breath. With the little strength he had left, Stuart threw his arm in the direction of Abe. Abe and Stuart locked arms and Abe pulled Stuart to safety. Both fell on the ground, breathing heavy, not able to talk.

Stuart sobbed as the reality of what just happened flooded him with emotion.

Once they could breathe normally again, Abe sat up and Stuart moved a bit to lean against a rock, wiping his face with his sleeves. Joshua handed them blankets and water. Then he walked about ten feet away and talked into his cell.

"Oh my God—I am sorry, I am so sorry," Linda cried as Frank wrapped a blanket around her as she sobbed.

After some time, a large jeep pulled up to take everyone else back to the base camp.

After everyone was seated in the jeep and Stuart settled down, Abe warmly looked at him. "So can you tell me what happened, bud?"

"Got me," answered Stuart. "I was walking around, taking in the scenery, and Linda appeared behind me. I guess it just scared me and I lost my footing."

Frank had his arm around Linda as she continued to cry.

Joshua spoke softly to the group, "Let's go back to our cabins, have a seat by the fire, and talk a bit." They rode in silence as they descended the mountain

As each member slowly exited the jeep, Joshua spoke, "This is the 'deeper in' part I was talking about in the cable car. Are you all ready for that?"

"Yes, absolutely," said Angela as they took their seats in the same chairs they sat in the evening before by the fire.

Stuart had just teetered on the brink of death and his eyes were now opened to the fact that he was not prepared to die after all and that if he was going to live, he needed to make some major changes. And he sensed the "deeper in" part he was about to embark on was just what he needed. He was all ears.

As they sat near the crackling fire, Joshua was silent, letting each person settle in.

"Stuart," said Linda in a soft voice. Her hands held her blanket up around her mouth. Before the words could come out, she sobbed uncontrollably. Everyone remained silent.

"I am so sorry," she finally said. "I walked over to you with every intention of flirting with you, knowing it was dangerous. Not just because we were on a mountain but for my marriage. But I did it anyway. And you almost died. I never meant any harm and I am so sorry. Will you forgive me?"

Stuart nodded and said, "I was not completely innocent either, Linda. I have this god awful history of dangerously flirting."

He snorted a mocking laugh. "I realized tonight how dangerous flirting is—literally!" He looked at Linda, "But thank you and yes, I do forgive you."

"Worse than that, I think I need to confess also that I am always doing that sort of flirting...it is like I need to control people or I have some sort of need for attention." She looked at Frank who sat straight up as he listened. "And I wonder why my husband walks in fear all the time? Frank, will you forgive me? You've lived with this garbage for 25 years, and you've never complained, you've always been so loving." She sobbed as Frank put his arm around her and rubbed her shoulder.

Joshua and the others remained silent.

Linda wiped her nose and snorted a little laugh, "I am sure Frank will be happy to hold me accountable not to do that again," she said as she moved slightly closer to Frank. Everyone let out a laugh and lightened the mood.

Joshua leaned into the group. "You know everyone here has issues or constraints. We've just begun to break through them. All of us want to be on track, on a path that leads to, oh, say a good life or perhaps even righteousness, right?"

Everyone nodded.

"None of us intend to do things like steal or get drunk, or have an affair—you pick whatever thing you think you will never do. We call it Neverland—I'll never cheat, I'll never lie-you've been there. All good intentions."

Stuart sat straight up in his chair. Grace, Preston, Angela, and Doug were resting, laid back, listening attentively. "So, you get married, you're going along and somewhere in there, you experience some form of rejection from your spouse and there are these ever so slight feelings of disconnect, whether it is physical or emotional. You with me?" He looked at everyone.

They nodded one by one.

"Okay, so little by little you feel more rejection at home, but you're not talking about it, mind you. You just push it down." Joshua continued.

"Then you are overwhelmed with responsibilities, there's more and more emotional or physical disconnect. Before you know it, you might be attracted to someone else."

Stuart started tapping his foot and wiping his brow. Abe's eyes shifted to Stuart.

"So, no big deal that you're attracted to someone, right? It's harmless, and you start fantasizing about that person. Again, perfectly harmless you think to yourself. You are not hurting anyone." Joshua looked at everyone and then at Abe.

"Before you know it, you have ended up off track. You think it doesn't look that far off base. You even justify to yourself you can get back on track yourself. But being off track "just a little" is a relative concept. Did you know that if the earth were slightly larger or smaller, human life could not exist? If the earth's speed were just slightly less than what it is, it would be gradually pulled toward the sun, eventually scorching and extinguishing life?"

"The fact is that being just slightly off track can eventually destroy us. We end up being separated from the right path or place where we believed we would never do things that would hurt us or worse, our loved ones!

"Where did we get off track?"

Doug said, "Right where we allowed rejection to come in."

"Bingo," Joshua said as he snapped his finger. "We start getting off track when we allow rejection to come in. And then there's a tiny crack that allows all sorts of things in—pride may be an issue, it gets in the way all the time. Fear and pride are dangerous—dangerous partners out to destroy us. Then they open the door for doubt, anger, lust, you name it. The key here folks is there may be something deep within us that needs healing.

"Now the goal of being on the path to righteousness is to be our **ideal self**. But realistically we find ourselves somewhere far below that, a place we call our **real self**.

"And the distance between our real selves and our ideal selves is directly correlated to the amount of stress we have in our lives. If I believe I am supposed to be a perfect faithful spouse but I have fallen way off track and am trying to live like everything is okay, then I am stressed. If I believe it is normal to work 60 hours a week, keep the house clean, have dinner ready and I am working 60 hours a week but not able to keep up with things . . . I am stressed. Multiply that by 20 times with all the things in our lives." He looked around at everyone, "Does this make sense?" Everyone slowly nodded.

"I think we can all agree we're a little stressed these days, right? And stress can have horrible effects on our bodies—in fact it can kill us!"

Everyone nodded.

"Okay, given that—then this teaching is about our physical being and let's imagine our bodies are like a gas tank.

> *The distance between our real selves and our ideal selves is directly linked to the amount of stress a person feels!*

"The top level is Serotonin. Like a car when the gas tank is full, everything is aligned, it runs smoother. When our level of serotonin is full we run smoother. When this starts to deplete we have problems with short-term memory. When we run out—our adrenals gets out of whack—that's when we dip into our Adrenaline level.

"When that happens, you can't sleep. You toss and turn. You're waking up, feeling tense you have a quick high, then a quick drop...then a real quick high, then a drop. Whew...you know what I'm talking about?

Everyone nodded. "Let's keep going. So when this level is depleted. . . .

"Anxiety kicks in. We start getting very anxious and this causes your heart to pump overtime. If you've ever felt like you've had a heart attack, it was an anxiety attack.

"Next, **Depression**." Angela's eyes brimmed with tears. "Your gas tank is depleted and depression appears to be a very normal state of mind to you. What you think is normal is *not* normal to others. It is very easy to slip into the next phase.

"Which are—Suicidal thoughts. This doesn't necessarily mean sticking a gun in your mouth or kicking a bucket from under your feet. This is when irrational thoughts occur, like thinking your family is better off without you. It can be anything you said you would never do.

"Any type of destructive behavior will destroy your family and behavior that will slowly kill you."

Angela patted her eyes as she openly cried.

Stuart was frozen in the words Joshua spoke.

"Now, we all have gas tank emptiers: activities or people we know that empty our tanks. And we all have gas tank fillers. Are you an emptier or a filler? Can you identify your emptiers and fillers? Sit down sometime, either alone or with your spouse, and list the things that fill and empty your tank. Once you understand what drains your tank, learn to know what fills your tank."

Angela nodded and dabbed her eyes again as Joshua asked, "So, what's the point of all this?"

Preston shrugged his shoulders. "That's easy! Seek the tank fillers and avoid the tank emptiers."

"Good job, Preston. *And*, we should commit to being with tank fillers. You have to be intentional about being a filler. This goes for your marriage, your business relationships, your friendships—any relationship."

Joshua remained silent for a moment. "From now on, be mindful of emptiers and fillers. Learn to identify when you are an emptier or with an emptier so you can change the focus to your fillers."

Angela continued to dry her eyes, "Joshua this is awesome," she blew her nose. "Heavy, but awesome. I think I'm going to have to turn in for the evening if that's okay with everyone. I have to think about this and clearly make some changes. I will see you in the morning," she said sleepily. "Oh wait!" She stopped, pulled out her intro card and handed it to Linda. "Just wanted you to have this."

Linda smiled and jumped up and hugged Angela who then shuffled off to her cabin.

"Gonna get a little shut eye as well," said Preston.

"Yep, me too," said Doug as he jumped to his feet. He reached out to shake Joshua's hand. "Thanks for today, Joshua. That was the best thing that has ever happened to me. Thanks for believing in me."

Joshua grabbed Doug's hand, looked him straight in the eye and said, "You did a great job tonight. The food was incredible—best I've ever eaten on this hike. Excellent job my friend. Or should I call you Determined Doug?"

Doug smiled. "Sure beats Doubtful, eh?" With that, he turned and jogged back to his cabin. Linda and Frank excused themselves as well after quietly waving goodnight.

Abe, Joshua and Stuart sat quietly for a few moments as the fire crackled and ember bits twisted through the air.

"Stuart," Joshua addressed Stuart firmly. "Any idea what happened tonight?"

Stuart shook his head, but his eyes were red and he held his hands close to his chin. "I have no idea, except I am on empty—and I am way off track." He swallowed hard. "I need help," he whispered.

Joshua patted his shoulder. "Do you think you are hovering at the depression or suicide level?"

"Yes," he could barely get the words out.

"Stuart, how will you stay on the track? How do you not allow your gas tank to deplete completely and slip into suicidal thoughts or actions?"

Stuart shrugged listlessly.

> **Gas Tank:**
> Serotonin Level
> Adrenaline Level
> Anxiety Level
> Depression Level
> Suicidal Level

"Try to keep you tank full. Exercise and eating well really do help fill up your gas tank. When you are at the bottom, you won't feel like exercising. You'll just fill up on junk food, because 'I deserve it . . . it makes me feel better.' This will not fill your gas tank.

"A key way to stay on the right path is to take the issues you are dealing with to 'bumper people.' Abe here is a classic bumper person for you because he is a friend who loves you and with whom you choose to be in relationship. You can share all your stuff, fears, hurts, and thoughts with him. He loves you enough to tell you when you are getting off track or BUMP you back on track. You can trust him enough to tell him when your heart is wandering and allow him to bump you.

"The number one reason people do not have bumper people is pride. Pride perpetuates the downward cycle. Our bumper people should be people who love us, who will share the 'lettuce in your teeth' moments of truth. This is different from accountability. This is a partnering ONLY because the person loves the person who needs counseling. Accountability might not be done out of a place of love but out of obligation instead. Learn to be honest and open and share with Abe."

"Wish I'd done that a long time ago," said Stuart hoarsely.

"Stuart, it is never too late. It's up to you how close you keep those bumper people. Some folks keep their bumper people way out here because they think it's safe," Joshua moved his arm way out to the side.

Stuart reflected on the fact that had he told Abe he was attracted to someone during a time when he struggled in his marriage, he wouldn't be where he was now. Instead, he didn't share because he didn't want to be judged.

"People think it's 'safe' to keep people at a distance—that's a lie. Share with one another and talk to each other; that's where the healing begins. If you think your marriage should be perfect and it isn't, you will be stressed—remember ideal self verses real self?"

Stuart was silent, watching Joshua.

"We live in fear, which causes us not to talk about our stuff. This fear usually goes all the way back to a place in our lives where there may have been some abuse, something happened that clearly was not our fault. But we don't want others to 'find out.' We live in fear, and the cycle begins. Fear opens the door to feeling weak, then shame sets in and then guilt. Before you know it—you are way off track.

"And as you confess it, the fear begins to go away. Are you catching this, buddy?"

Stuart slowly nodded. "It's a process, right" He looked at Abe. "Abe, you and I have almost exactly the same pasts. Right down to a tee. I can't believe all the times you reached out to me I never reciprocated in sharing my childhood stuff with you."

Abe reached out and patted his arm, "No worries bud, really!! In fact, I shared my past the same time I talked to you about hippocampus—you just weren't ready to hear it. I think you are now!"

Joshua waited and then spoke. "Stuart, you have a good friend here. Let him help you . . . talk to Abe, make him your bumper person. Don't carry around a bunch of secrets! When you live your life like this, Stuart, many people around you will need that same healing and you—yes, you, Stuart, can become a messenger of hope."

Joshua was silent as he watched Stuart stare at the fire. Without a word, Stuart reached in his pocket and gave Abe his introduction card. Abe quietly took it and leaned back in his chair. The three men sat in silence together

Bumper People:
People we trust who love us and will share the truth!

"Stuart," Joshua finally said softly. "Would you like to pray?"

Stuart stared at Joshua for a long time and then closed his eyes. The fire popped as embers drifted upward. The three men bowed their heads and prayed.

CHAPTER TWENTY-TWO:

Freedom in Forgiveness

Joshua and Abe headed to the patio for the last breakfast they would have with the team. When they reached the patio, they saw Grace and Angela having a lively conversation and Stuart standing with his back toward them, looking out over the mountains and valleys.

"Good morning, Stuart," said Joshua in his usual jovial, booming voice.

Stuart turned with a start. "Good morning, guys!" He said as he walked over to them. He had a bounce in his walk, his shoulders were straight, and his eyes glistened with life. He smiled as he reached out to shake their hands but then changed his mind and reached out for a hug. Hugging Joshua was like hugging a bear, and they laughed with a deeper level of care and compassion. Then he turned to hug Abe as well. Grace and Angela hugged Abe and Joshua as well.

"Wow, I cannot thank you guys enough for last night. You both saved my life—literally! That was powerful! First of all for rescuing me! I could have died! And then giving me a second chance at life by sharing with me about the gas tank and Neverland! Wow—Josh, you should write a book!"

"Hey, are we missing something?" asked Linda and Frank as they arrived. They reached out to hug everyone as well.

Preston and Doug came and were greeted in the same way. Everyone grabbed a plate and settled in to eat, savoring every morsel of food as well as time with their friends.

"So, tell me something good," Joshua said.

"I had the best night's sleep of my life," said Stuart.

"I agree," chimed Angela. "This was the most restful time I've ever enjoyed. But I am curious, what were you guys talking about? Did we miss anything good after we retired last night?"

"Well, only the most important part of the whole hike," joked Stuart.

"Tell us about it. We want to know too," said Preston as he and Doug walked in.

Joshua spoke as he jumped up to get another piece of toast. "That's a great idea, Angela. In fact, Stuart, why don't you share with them what you learned about bumper people last night and anything else you want to share? You know you retain 90% of the information you learn when you turn right around and teach it to another!"

Stuart leaned back in his chair and started sharing. "Well, okay. All of us struggle with something and when we do, we need to take it to our bumper people. A bumper person is a friend who loves us and with whom we choose to be in a relationship. They are someone with whom you can share your fears, hurts, and thoughts. They love us enough to tell us when we are getting off track and they BUMP us back on track. You trust them enough to tell them when your heart is wandering and allow them to bump you.

"And we have to learn to be honest, open, and share with at least one bumper person." Stuart looked over at Joshua, "We constantly live in fear, shame and guilt." Stuart's voice started to shake as he worked at composing himself. "The minute you confess it, the fear goes away." He closed his eyes and stopped talking.

"Sorry," he raised his hand. "Clearly, I have a lot more to learn in this area."

Preston coughed, and then said, "Well, a huge thanks to Joshua for that teaching. That information was really helpful. In fact, it took awhile for me to fall asleep because I was going over the gas tank. That was huge. It was an eye opener for me because I believe that not dealing with our constraints makes us sink to the bottom of that gas tank really easily," he said as he sat up quickly.

"Wow!" said Preston as he shook his head.

"What," asked Joshua?

"Well, I have been in business all my life and I just now realized how much easier it is to understand constraints and explain it because of what I've learned on this hike."

"What do you think the difference is," asked Stuart, genuinely interested in hearing what Preston had to say.

"I realize that the biggest constraint for me is...pride!" Preston lowered his head. "I always act like I know more than everyone else. Geez, I could go on for days explaining and identifying my pride issues." He slowly nodded his head as he looked out beyond the group. "Now I get it; no organization, or family, team, church, or any other group can get beyond the constraints of its leadership, policies or processes."

Oh," he sat up quickly, "I figured something else out, and I want to see if I am correct."

"Okay," said Joshua with raised eyebrows.

"I now understand why you put Linda up front to lead the group as we hiked."

"You do, eh?"

He looked at Linda, "I hope this isn't an insult to you."

Linda shook her head side to side, "Absolutely not. I am curious as well. Please continue."

"Well, Linda was somewhat of a constraint to our group in that she was the slowest walker, which caused everyone following her to slow down, and separated our team, right?

"When Linda was in front, our team could only go as fast as the leader. Just the fact that everyone from the team was walking behind her made her pick up her pace." Preston looked at Linda, "Did you feel that? Like you wanted to walk faster because others were behind you who were walking fast?"

She smiled, "Yes, in fact, you're right! That's why I was concerned about leading the group. I knew I had to step up to the plate on a consistent basis."

Preston nodded in agreement, and looked at Joshua. "She wasn't given the opportunity to slack off like she could when she was in the middle of the pack." said Preston as he shook his head.

"You do get it. Preston, thanks for sharing. I know it took a lot to say that. You know, folks, most of us deal with the very same pride issues that

Preston just talked about. But there is also something else very common in all of us. There's one constraint that many of us come up against in our own lives. If we are unforgiving, it will destroy relationships and fester mistrust. It is rooted in pride.

"Many of us not only harbor lack of forgiveness toward others, we've not forgiven ourselves. We blame ourselves for things we are not responsible for. People who have been sexually abused think they did something as a child to warrant that abuse. That's a lie. Remember, the abuse was real. It really happened. It is the lie associated with the truth that folks continue to carry throughout their lives.

"We are only limited by the lies we believe to be true in our lives. As adults, these lies manifest in us as constraints that hold us back—fear, pride, anger, lust, and doubt.

"Not many of us walk in the freedom of forgiveness because we've not forgiven others. We say we have, but we really have not. And we hold those grudges, deep down inside." Joshua paused longer than his normal uncomfortable pause as he watched everyone. He spoke softly, "If there is someone for whom you need to ask forgiveness, don't think too long. Just go and ask. It will give you so much freedom, peace, and break through a constraint I'll bet you didn't even know you had.

Joshua turned and locked eyes with Preston. "Preston, remember we changed your name—from Prideful Preston to Perceptive Preston" asked Joshua.

"Yeah, I remember—thanks." He flashed a boyish grin as his eyes brightened.

Grace stood to talk. "Folks, I almost forgot—here is a little gift for you to help you remember self identity, remember when we talked about that? It's a chain."

"Yes," said Preston as he held it up, "with a conspicuous missing link. Umm, I'm curious!" He lowered his arm and looked at grace.

> *Many of us not only harbor lack of forgiveness toward others, we've not forgiven ourselves. We blame ourselves for things we are not responsible for.*

"Very perceptive of you Perceptive Preston. It is a missing link—you'll have to find that link."

"Excellent," said Preston.

Grace held her hands together by her chin, her eyes were filled with joy, yet were tearful. "This is where I say good bye. I've enjoyed being part of your group and I am so blessed that I got to see your lives transform right before my eyes—wow! What an incredible group. Please keep in touch with me and I love you all. I hope you enjoy the rest of the hike, and be careful going home."

Angela stood. "Grace, I've learned so much from you. Thank you for sharing your story." She held her hand over her mouth as she chuckled. "At first I thought you were a little too happy for me. Then as I watched you and heard you share, I realized it wasn't happiness at all. It was real joy— the kind of joy I want in my life. Thank you for showing me what joy looks like." She reached out to hug Grace.

Abe walked up to Grace and gave her a huge bear hug as did everyone else. Grace wiped away a tear as she turned to Joshua.

"So long, my friend. It is always good to spend time with you."

Joshua wrapped his arms around Grace and they embraced for a long time. "Thanks so much for sharing," he said as he hugged her. "I'm sad I won't see you for awhile!"

"I'm not," Grace laughed. "I'll be basking in the sun in Italy for awhile. I can't wait. Love you, my friend."

"Love you too," said Joshua as he choked back his tears.

Doug jumped up to give Grace a hug. He said something to her and then turned to the group. "Grace made a great suggestion to us about the cards, some of us have already given our cards away. So on behalf of Grace, I want to give Stuart my card."

Doug walked over to Frank and held out his hand. "Frank, thanks for being so transparent. To see you and Linda change so much, and I know there's a lot to work on, but you are an encouragement to me and I want to stay in touch. I hope by my giving you this card, you will reach out to me."

Stuart stood and gave Doug a hug, surprised by his own actions and desires to be real with the people he called friend.

Preston jumped up. "Great reminder, Doug. And I'd like to give you mine." The two men smiled and turned to look at Joshua as he addressed the group.

"Well," Joshua turned and faced the group and clapped his hands. "We've got a bit of a hike to get back to headquarters, so let's head out. The staff will pick up your gear at your cabin and meet us at headquarters." With that he pounded the stick and started walking.

"I'm going to miss this place," said Angela.

"Me too," said Linda as she smiled at Angela. Everyone nodded in agreement as they fell into line behind Joshua and waved goodbye to Grace!

They walked for several hours, sometimes in silence, other times in lively conversation. They took one break before they arrived at the cabin Joshua called 'headquarters'. "Folks, grab a box lunch, some water, and come on over here and sit with me for a bit."

They sat in the same spot where they were when they first met.

"How 'bout some affirmations!"

Angela almost jumped out of her seat. "Oh, Doug, you made a fabulous dinner last night and I really enjoyed it! Thank you for that treat. You really came out of your shell last night and there is such a difference in you, you're like a new person."

Doug beamed as he described his renewed sense of purpose in having the opportunity to work with a couple of top chefs.

"Angela," Preston said. "Thank you for sharing about your father. You are a different person today than you were four days ago. The transformation is just unbelievable. You are a warm, loving, caring person who brought a real sense of joy to the group. Thanks for being with us."

"Why, thank *you*, Preston!" She crinkled her nose as she smiled and her eyes danced.

Abe took off his hat and shook the dust off. As he brushed his hair back he looked at Preston. "Preston, I think you are one of the smartest people I know. Really, I've never met anyone like you. When you admitted the constraint of pride that you deal with, it's like the shackles were broken. I mean, even your face lit up. It was like all the wisdom you have is multiplied a hundredfold because it is coupled with a sense of peace from God. You don't have to prove anything any longer. You are free to be who God created you to be. And there is real joy in that!" He reached in his pocket and handed Preston his intro card. "I hope we remain good friends for years to come."

Preston threw his head back and laughed. It was contagious. "Absolutely we will," he said as he reached for the card.

> *"When you admit the constraint of pride that you deal with, the shackles are broken."*

Stuart dabbed his eyes as he tried to speak. His mouth opened but he couldn't form any words. Abe grabbed Stuart's shoulder as he watched his friend. Stuart looked at Abe and said, "I—I don't even know what to say. Since I have known you, you have been my pillar of strength, as much as I would let you, anyway. I have counted on you for so many things and you have been there. You have been a good friend. But what you did for me last night was above and beyond the call of duty. You," he stopped. "Literally," he stopped again. Finally he whispered, "saved my life!" He choked back the tears. "How on earth do I thank you for that? And when you and Joshua challenged me on being depressed, you hit the nail on the head. Thank you for challenging me." He wiped his eyes with his sleeve. "You have been a dear friend!"

There was not a dry eye in the group. They sat in silence for several moments, but then the affirmations popped up all over the place for Joshua, Abe and everyone on the team.

"As we're getting ready to pack up our cars and head back home, let me share some final words with you all. It was a great experience up on the mountain top, wasn't it?"

Everyone nodded with enthusiasm. Joshua put his hands together. "But I don't believe we were created for mountain top experiences. They are merely times of respite, times of inspiration. It's what you do in the valley that counts." Joshua pointed to the very tip of the mountains, "It's what you take from the mountain top, the inspiration you receive up there, and how you use it down there," he pointed to the valley. "I once read that the mountaintop is not meant to teach us something, it is meant to *make* us something. So let me ask you—on this hike, were you taught or were you transformed?"

Angela swallowed, "Definitely transformed."

"Me too," the others agreed.

Joshua took out the covenant.

"Then let me ask you to do something. Don't merely think about what you did, use the tools we've given you and refer often to this." He held up the covenant. "Go through that exercise with your family and your team."

Everyone nodded in agreement.

"Now, tell me quickly, what is the one thing you learned during our time together that you are going to change or apply in your life going forward. Quick, right off the top of your head, what is it?" Joshua looked at Angela.

"I'm going to go to my mom," said Angela as she wiped her eyes, "and ask her to forgive me for the anger I've stored up all these years because I didn't grieve for my dad. And I hope that is the start of dealing with my anger issues."

Preston raised his hand next. "I'm going to ask my team at work to forgive me for being so arrogant and prideful." He looked up and his face brightened. "I am also going to share the information that I learned, walk through the covenant process, and ask how I can serve them."

Doug smiled and said, "I'm going to compete for a spot on Food Network's Top Chef Show." He laughed out loud as everyone joined in. "No, really, I am going to check out the culinary classes at the college. I understand we have a pretty decent school. I no longer doubt that I can be a good chef and I am willing to work hard to hone my skills."

He shuffled his feet in the sand and looked up as a tear trickled down the side of his nose. "I need to work on my marriage too. It's worth working on and I know a few bumper people I need to connect and also get some professional help. I think my wife will be amazed when I suggest this. But it will take some work."

Everyone clapped heartily.

"Good job, Doug," Frank said as he turned to look at Linda. "We're committed also to getting help and working on our marriage. We both contributed to its downfall and we both want to make it work. It was really helpful to learn where all my fear originated from as a kid. I never shared with anyone—not even Linda—about the abuse. Now that I've shared it with her, we can get beyond my horrible self identity and begin to work on a healthier version of me."

Linda had her head down but as she lifted her face it was brighter than the sun. She smiled and said, "I need to let some things go in my past. You don't have to have a really horrible past or childhood to wallow in crud... it's just there. So I probably need to forgive a few folks. And I need to go to my dad and ask for forgiveness for the pain I've caused him. There are so many folks I need to forgive or ask their forgiveness, which I've already done with my husband." When Frank looked at her, she released a cheerful laugh.

Joshua's eyes danced as he watched a different couple share their hearts.

"Linda, what was the name you started with"

"Oh," she waved her hand, "Luscious—pretty typical, eh?"

"So what do you say to a new name?"

"Oh wait," interrupted Angela as she jumped up. "Let me give her the new name," she said eagerly.

Linda clapped her hands and smiled widely as she anxiously awaited to be gifted with a new name.

Angela stood tall and opened her arms wide, "Ladies and gentlemen, I give you the new, improved, Laughing Linda!"

Linda threw her head back as she laughed like a little girl. "Wow, I do feel so much lighter and freer." She looked at Angela and bowed her head. "Thank you so much! Oh and here!" She handed Angela her intro card and they exchanged hugs.

Joshua put his foot up on a rock and leaned on his knee. "Now that's awesome stuff, thanks ladies!"

"Stuart, how about you?"

"I've learned that personal transformation is the key. It's important to dig down deep and get the little hidden things out. It's also important to understand where those things come from. From my childhood which was abusive—I ran away at a young age to living a lie most of my adult years. I don't want to live in that guilt and shame anymore.

"Hiking with you folks has taught me a lot. While it may be difficult initially to be transparent, I plan on doing so going forward. Starting with my wife...somehow." He laughed a nervous laugh. "Not sure how yet, and I hope I can teach my kids to be transparent so they don't have to walk around trying to bury their crud and then they can teach their kids. It's all about walking this out, being free and passing this on to others so they can have the same freedom."

Abe interrupted. "And I'm going to be a better bumper person, starting with Stuart!"

"Excellent," said Joshua. "You are all off to a wonderful start. Please keep it up. Remember when the pressure's off we tend to go to where???"

"Into the box!!"

"So do you believe if you apply one tool every day, your life will be different? And hopefully that one tool is just a start. Do you have the tools you need to see transformation in your lives?"

"Yes," everyone laughed as they zipped up their bags, stuffed things in one side, juggled, and shifted weight around.

Preston raised his hand as he dangled the chain with the missing link. "Hey, so what's the missing link?"

"Oh, I almost forgot. Thanks Preston." Joshua reached into his pocket and pulled out a velvet blue bag. He handed each member a gold ring that fit perfectly into the place of the missing link. Upon closer examination, the inside of the ring had a beautiful script that read, "Personal Transformation. Pass it on!"

Joshua whispered, "Ponder those words. God bless you all!"

The team hugged, and shed tears. By the time they finished their farewells, every single person felt the effects of the sincere affirmations they had received.

Abe slapped Stuart on the back. "Ready, bud?"

Stuart pulled the string to his bag and hoisted it over his shoulder. "Yep, let's roll."

Joshua called after Stuart. "Stuart, buddy, we didn't give you a new name!"

With his hand on the car door handle and a boyish grin across his face, Stuart looked back at Joshua. "How about Simply Stuart?"

Joshua smiled, "I like it!"

Joshua watched as everyone drove away, waving as the dust billowed high above him.

"I'll really miss them," he whispered out loud as the last car drove out of sight.

CHAPTER TWENTY THREE:

Launching

Stuart was quiet as he drove Abe to his home.

"You doing okay?" Abe asked as he studied Stuart's face.

Stuart pursed his lips and shook his head no. "That part about confessing? Well, I have to confess something."

He looked at Abe, who had the warm, gentle smile of a true friend.

"I have been fired from my job as CEO and I have been having an affair."

Once again he looked at Abe, expecting to see judgment, but still Abe's face showed warmth, love and no sign of judgment.

Stuart poured his heart out for the next forty-five minutes about how far off track he was from Neverland. Abe listened as the loving friend he was. He also asked some very pointed questions to challenge Stuart.

"Have you told Jill?"

"No. Geez. She'd kill me. You mean about the job or the affair?"

Abe just looked at Stuart and Stuart answered his own question. "No. I'll have to figure out something. No way can I tell her. She would die inside and I just couldn't do that to her."

"But you could have an affair?"

"Yeah. I see what you're getting at Abe and I know you're right. I'm just not sure I can."

"Stuart, have you ever thought about what Jill needs?"

"Well," he shrugged. "Sort of."

"I might be guessing here, but I'll bet you think this other woman gave you the respect you were searching for, correct?"

"Well, as pathetic as it sounds, yeah."

"And all this time, Jill needs love and you're not providing it for her."

"Well, I am providing a good home and life and she really needs that. That's the way I show her I love her."

"Well, how's that workin' for you, my friend?"

Stuart slumped his shoulders as he stared ahead.

Abe remained silent as he watched Stuart process. "Here's a thought, Stuart. Tell me if this is right. Men don't feel respected, so they shut down; and women don't feel loved, so they 'nitpick.' Nitpicking causes further feelings of disrespect, so men withdraw even more; and women feel more unloved when a man withdraws. If a man shows love, maybe the cycle would change, but over time, not overnight. The more a man shows true, genuine love, the better the chance that respect will be returned to him. Hang in there with Jill, and change the cycle. If you continue to show Jill the love she needs, each time something happens that may send her back into the "no respect" mode, she might not go as far back as she may have when you were not giving her any love. Until that day when there is no going back. And that day is possible if you choose to give Jill the love she needs. And it all starts with?"

"Me confessing?"

"Yep!"

"So are you saying I should confess all this to her, just like that?"

"Is there any other way? What's holding you back?"

"Fear!"

"Of what?"

"Losing her and my kids," said Stuart.

Stuart looked at Abe and then back at the road. He kept his eyes focused on the lines on the street.

Finally, Abe spoke. "Stuart, what's the right thing to do?"

"Be honest and confess everything to her," Stuart whispered.

"What else?"

"Saying I'm sorry and asking for forgiveness?" Stuart felt a twinge of pain mixed with a lighthearted feeling as he spoke those words and turned down the street where Abe lived.

"Bingo. There is no better way to be free," Abe said as Stuart put the car in park. They sat in Abe's driveway for another hour as they discussed how having Abe as a bumper person would benefit Stuart so that he would never listen to the dark voice again. Finally, the two men got out of the car to unload Abe's gear.

As they hugged and said goodbye, Stuart looked at Abe and said, "Abe, you are a good man. Thanks for hanging in there with me."

"You're certainly welcome. Now about that confession—I'll call you in a couple days to check on how you did."

"Uh, yeah. You can call and check. Not sure I will have done anything, but yeah."

That thought began to nestle into Stuart's soul—*Abe is going to call me this week and what am I going to say? Why wait? Just do the right thing.*

The sun was barely visible over the distant mountains where they had hiked the last few days. As he pulled into his drive, he saw Jill and the children through the window in the dining room, just finishing bedtime snacks. He had called her when he left Abe's to let her know he was on his way home. They had not talked since he'd left for the hike. He felt he couldn't get out of the car fast enough to be with them again. Warmth rushed over him as he walked through the door, dropped his gear, and knelt down with the kids and hugged them so tight that his young son took it as a challenge and tried to out squeeze his dad. He fought back the tears and finally stood up. He pulled Jill close to him and kissed her, whispering, "I missed you!"

She pulled back and looked at him with a slight grin. "You okay?"

"Yeah, yeah. I'm good." As the kids ran upstairs to bed, Jill called after them. "Make sure you brush your teeth, you two. I'll—we'll be right up to tuck you in," she turned to Stuart and winked. Stuart slumped into the oversized armchair, closed his eyes, and let out a long sigh.

He waited a minute, trying to pretend all was well. Jill continued to watch him. Then he began, "I have something to share with you."

Jill bit her lower lip and nodded. "Let's get the kids to bed and we'll relax and talk." She peered into his face and he knew she was looking for clues as to what he was thinking.

Once the children were in bed and all was quiet, the time had come. There were no more excuses, no more delays, and no more justifications. Just Stuart and Jill...face to face. Stuart poured out everything from the job to the suicide attempt to the affair to the transformational hike. Jill listened.

As he watched her, he was amazed at the serene look on her face. It scared him. Stuart grabbed her hand and looked into her eyes. "Jill, I am so sorry for everything. Will you forgive me?"

Jill sat in silence.

Stuart nervously continued, "I know our marriage may be over and I don't expect you to forgive me. I don't know how you could even love me. Forgiving me seems almost impossible."

Jill dropped her head as a tear rolled from the side of her cheek into her lap. He waited as his heart was sure to burst through his shirt. And he waited.

As she raised her head, tears had traced down her cheek on the same path so many tears had traveled before. Swallowing hard, she said, "Why would I leave you, Stuart? Yes, I forgive you! I love you more than anything else on earth."

Stuart grasped her hands as he sobbed. He struggled to believe his wife could forgive him for the things he did, knowing he didn't deserve her love. The minute he looked into her eyes—he knew he was indeed forgiven. The dark voice was shattered forever. The still small voice that was squelched for so many years arose as he heard once again, "Well done!"

THE REST OF THE STORY

Dan was resting against the back of his chair when Ford stopped speaking.

"So, is that it? She just forgave him, just like that?" He was not ready for the story to be over.

"Well," Ford said in a matter-of-fact manner. "Yes, she forgave him—but it was a process, remember? Not an event. They had a lot of work to do. The hike had churned up enough crud inside for him to be able to initiate the work they should have done a long time ago."

Dan had many more questions. "So, do I know this Stuart?"

"You might. What do you think?"

Dan laughed as he said, "At one point I thought Stuart might have actually been you, but then when I heard you describe Abe, the really good friend, I thought, 'hmm, maybe he's Abe.' Not sure why I think you had to be any of them, but then I finally figured out you were Joshua." When Dan pushed, Ford lovingly pushed back.

Ford shrugged, "Whatever you think, Dan. Could be all three, could be none. That's for you to decide."

"Okay, one more question. Before you shared the story you said your friend, Stuart, found the missing link...was it really just personal transformation?"

Ford looked at Dan and asked, "What do you think it is?"

Dan kept waiting for the one big key as Ford shard and then, BAM! His face lit up. "So the entire hike was more about transformation than it was leadership—"

"You can't get to that level of leadership or see a city or organization transformed unless each individual is willing to experience deep personal transformation."

"Right, and with that personal transformation comes the need, or desire I should say, to want to pour into other people's lives so they can experience personal transformation, right?"

"Bingo! You've got it!

"Really? Well, can you tell me more about how Stuart and Jill worked it out?"

Ford glanced at his watch, slung his backpack over his shoulder and turned to give Dan a hug.

"Perhaps another time, Dan, there is definitely more to the story. Let's just suffice it to say that if he had known what some of the consequences were to his actions…he would have never made the mistakes he made."

As the door closed behind Ford, Dan looked forward to hearing more of the story for he knew he was ready for the next level of transformation.

AFFIRMATIONS

Thank you to all the folks who have attended training sessions over the years. The feedback we have received from you has been incredible. Because of your willingness to apply what you've learned, we have been blessed beyond belief. Thank you to each of you who have shared how your lives have been transformed.

Thank you to Michael McClellan for your willingness to read each version carefully. You lovingly pointed out the necessary edits and gave us so much incredible wisdom. To Deborah Adleman, Maryam Kubasek and Paula Bussard who have poured over each word and lent us their editing skills and talents. Thank you, Dan McNeil. This book would not be possible without your love and support!

From Ford: To my three lovely daughters; Whitney, Emily and Quincy. My role as a father has taught me so much more than any book or job title ever could. Your love for me in spite of myself has helped me to see and understand the unconditional love God has for me. I thank God for you and am filled with joy every second I think of you. To Sandra: I cannot express what I feel in my heart for you. Your love through these years in spite of my failings as a husband has spurred me on to be the man I am today. While I have been teaching this material, you have been walking it out. Your support has been my rock to stand on and your love is the place I take comfort and rest. Thank you for loving me and believing in me.

From Danise:

Thank you to my wonderful family for always loving and supporting me. To Marisa and Matt and for my precious granddaughter, Evi Isabella—you are gas tank fillers! My prayer is that this book enlightens each of us to be more loving and better people—starting with me!

ABOUT THE AUTHORS

Danise DiStasi
Danise spent 27 years in the medical industry. She has held positions including Nuclear Product Specialist, Corporate Account Manager and Vice President of Sales and Marketing. In 2000, she left the medical industry and joined the Ken Blanchard Companies as well as Lead Like Jesus, a business ministry co-founded by Ken Blanchard and Phil Hodges. In 2005 she joined FSH Consulting Group as a facilitator, trainer, speaker, author, and coach. Her mission is to spur people on in their quest to seek personal transformation through training, coaching, speaking and personal mentoring.

Ford Taylor
Ford owned and operated an apparel company which he grew from a small enterprise to a large publicly traded corporation. After many years as a corporate leader, he left that role and became an executive leadership consultant, specializing in acquisitions, turnarounds, mergers and leadership development beginning with participants understanding personal constraints. He started FSH Consulting group which continues to grow and is based in Cincinnati, OH.

FOR MORE INFORMATION ON THE TRAINING/COACHING, DVD MATERIAL AND OTHER BUSINESS SERVICES PROVIDED BY FSH CONSULTING GROUP:
Visit our website: www.transformlead.com
Or email us at: danise@transformlead.com
Or call: 513 477.7624

WHAT OTHERS ARE SAYING

Transformational Leadership is one of the most valuable investments of three days I have ever made into helping me become a better leader. Understanding the balance between relational and transactional leadership was worth the entire three days. If you lead others, you can not afford to miss this training.

- Os Hillman, President, <u>Marketplace Leaders</u>;
Author, *TGIF* and *The 9 to 5 Window*

Our company grew from $3.7 million to $7.2 million in one year. Without the training, we would have imploded rather than experiencing incredible growth. Not only that, our employees have seen a difference in their personal lives as well.

- Dan McNeil, President & Co-Owner, <u>Apex Restoration</u>

The training taught me the difficult lessons of change. People SELDOM change until the pain of staying the same exceeds the pain of change. I left Transformational Leadership with stretch marks! You will also. They are worth it.

- Terry Nelson, President, Urban Leadership University

My business increased in worth by almost 2.5 times the amount it was valued at just prior to this training due to the positive changes we saw take place in our team. But more importantly, families have been restored as a result of this training. We are very grateful and blessed.

- Randy Murgittroyd, Owner, Subway franchises

Transformational Leadership gave me a tool set to achieve that sweet spot of convergence between relationship and transaction in both business and personal inter-actions. Encouraged by trainers who lead by example, this was a life-changing experience that I recommend to anyone desiring to step up their game.

- Michelle Titus, Principal, Michelle Titus & Associates

I was so impacted by Transformational Leadership that I decided to move to Cincinnati to become the COO of a private equity fund that uses the principles of Transformational Leadership to turn around businesses.

- Michael McClellan, COO, TOF

If you are a leader who wants to see reformation of your team, if you desire more unity and oneness within your team, if you would like to see sound conflict resolution principles set in your team, I recommend this training.

- Jerry Culbreth, Pastor, <u>Tryed Stone New Beginning Church</u>

This training has transformed my life and company. A couple big ideas for me were the power of living a transparent life and affirmations. When we began using affirmations in our company there were tears flowing in the room.

- Glenn Repple, President, <u>G A Repple and Company</u>

The training enabled us to understand a vital key to success in our business operations: the value of relationships. We recommend Transformational Leadership to every business owner with a vision to grow and succeed.

- Steve and Vareena Swihart, Owners, <u>Swihart Industries</u>

The experiential learning helped me understand how I show up and give myself to those that I lead in my professional life and those that I love in my personal life. I wholeheartedly encourage EVERY marketplace leader to invest in themselves by going through Transformational Leadership training!

- Tom Stansbury, Entrepreneur-In-Residence,
<u>Regent University Center for Entrepreneurship</u>

I thought that I'd let you know that we've made some really cool progress with our team since the training. We could have never come this far toward becoming a functional team without the week that we spent with you. Amazing. I had a wonderful week with you in Cincinnati. My whole team is changed.

- Dr. Patrick Murray, Senior Pastor, <u>The Living Word Church</u>

The Transformational Leadership Training triggered, both in myself and those that I work with, new ways to look at how we go about 'doing business' by removing constraints and replacing them with healing and healthy alternatives. It is well worth the time!"

- Rob Stease, CEO, <u>Honeymoon Paper Products</u>

My partner and I have chosen to run our business based on the principles we learned in training. Transformational Leadership is not for the faint of heart. It was, however, three days that changed my life.

- Richard Cole, CEO and Managing Member,
Green Global Holdings, LLC

The Transformational Leadership course was both a self examination and an active participation of God working through thought leadership to bless people in my life and ministry.

- Max Hooper, President, <u>Vision 360</u>

STUDY GUIDE

CHAPTER ONE: *The Suicidal C.E.O*

What were all the issues Stuart was dealing with?

_____

What was the final breaking point for him:

_____

Can you relate, even slightly, to Stuart's despair?

_____

CHAPTER TWO: *The Dark Voice*

What was the purpose behind Stuart's dark voice?

_____

Do people really experience hearing voices like that?

_____

CHAPTER THREE: *Tell me something good!*

Now be honest, when Joshua first opened their time together with this line, did you ask yourself…"What are they doing?"

Next time you are with a group, ask the group to tell you something good! What happened?

_____

_____

CHAPTER FOUR: *Getting to know you!*
CHAPTER FIVE: *Are we who we say we are?*

Next time you are with someone new or a new group, share these three things:
Who I am, what I do and why I'm here!

_____

In your mind, could you imagine each character as they shared their names and stories?

_____

What were some of the issues each person dealt with?

_____

Can you relate to any of the names or constraints?

_____

CHAPTER SIX: *Affirmations*

This was your favorite part, right? Well, okay…maybe it seemed a bit awkward for the hiking group who just met. Speaking positive affirmations to each other is a very powerful tool, not only at work, but in your personal life as well. The steps of an affirmation are:

• Look at the person you want to affirm and, using "I—you" language, affirm them and sincerely thank them.

- Try not to use, "I **want** to thank"...or "I **want** to affirm..." Many people get up and give acceptance speeches and say, "I want to thank my Mom and Dad..." when their mom and dad are sitting right there...so just thank them!

Write an affirmation for someone you know who may need this encouragement.

_____

_____

_____

Now go to them and give them this gift. Affirm them and watch how they light up.

How did you feel when you affirmed that person?

_____

_____

How does it make you feel when you receive an affirmation?

_____

_____

The ability to affirm others is a necessary skill that is learned. It is imperative that we practice this skill regularly. Why aren't we doing this in our businesses or at home for that matter?

_____

_____

Joshua spoke briefly about being relational and transactional. What were your thoughts as he challenged the group to be more relational before jumping into transactions?

_____

_____

Being relational and speaking affirmations to each other may be uncomfortable at first, but try it and see what transpires. Imagine how different our organizations, work places and families would be if we made this one change and sincerely affirmed people on a regular basis? Your transactions will be healthier if first rooted in trusting relationships.

Practice affirmations on a regular basis!

CHAPTER SEVEN: *Social Anxiety*

The majority of hikers felt some level of anxiety as they started out. These are the same fears that affect the performance of many teams.

Social Anxiety is made up of:

_____   +   _____

What causes us to be fearful? List as many things as you can. List the fears you have.

_____

_____

Why do we need to understand social anxiety?

_____

_____

What are some specific things you can do to reduce the level of anxiety people feel in your environment?

_____

_____

CHAPTER EIGHT: *The Power of Forgiveness*

We believe the covenant process is one of the most important tools to use in your organization or family.

The team discussed the following questions:

1. When we're together, how do we want to treat each other?
2. Assuming we agree on how to treat each other (question #1), what will we do if one of us does not follow the behavior we agreed upon?

The question came up that the team discussed in detail: Does this refer to this group or our work or employees? What do you think?

_____

_____

List as many behaviors as you can (without looking) which the team agreed to in their covenant.

_____

_____

Grace shared a powerful story about forgiveness. What were your thoughts as she shared? What steps did she take to offer an apology?

_____

_____

If there is someone you need to ask forgiveness of, write some thoughts about what you might want to say to them. What steps do _you_ need to take to offer an apology? (Personalize the steps).

_____

_____

CHAPTER NINE: _What does the Covenant Say?_

How did the team decide to resolve conflict? What steps did they agree to take for conflict resolution?

_____

_____

_____

Why did Stuart and Preston have such a hard time resolving such a small issue? What stood in the way?

_____

_____

It takes strength to care about people and to acknowledge and address conflict. Leaders must be strong enough to put a covenant agreement into place and walk it out.

CHAPTER TEN: *It's a Process*

What would have happened if Joshua told the team how to behave with each other? Why didn't he hand them a set of rules?

Tell me..._____
Teach me..._____
Involve me...._____

Think of a time when you needed to be involved in learning a skill as opposed to just being told. What happened?

_____

_____

What happens to our motivation to learn when we are "told" to do something?

_____

_____

How does this relate to the motivation of your team or even your marriage or personal relationships?

_____

_____

CHAPTER ELEVEN: *What's a Hippocampus?*

The **hippocampus** is a part of the brain located inside the temporal lobe and plays a part in memory and navigation. The name derives from its curved shape, which slightly resembles a seahorse (Greek: hippocampus). The hippocampus is known to be associated with memories of personally experienced events and their associated emotions.

When an event takes place, it actually goes through a series of processes before it is stored in the memory part of the hippocampus and then transferred into the longer-term memory banks of the cerebral cortex or better known as cognitive thinking. An interaction can be short and somewhat emotionally charged. Such events can travel up the brain stem and "park" at the door of the hippocampus.

In order to enter the hippocampus, an event has to have two things associated with it;

_____ and _____

Over time if an event is repeated in the same format, the noted information is transferred to the cerebral cortex and stored as a substantive thought. The effect is that whenever anything that is closely related to a past learning experience occurs, the same response is forthcoming.

People respond to _____ *out of their* _____ *experiences.*

Think of ways you can be more aware of how people respond to current situations based on their past experiences.

_____

_____

Discuss with your group or bumper person things that you believe are in your hippocampus that might be constraints to your being a better leader, person, husband, wife, etc.

_____

_____

CHAPTER TWELVE:

The Pain of Change…we either love it or hate it!

Joshua said Change SELDOM occurs until the pain of staying the same exceeds the pain of change.

What are the steps to processing change?

_____

_____

Do you agree with the statement, "No organization can get beyond the constraints of its leadership, policies or processes?" Can you think of some examples of how this plays out in your organization or family?

_____

_____

We are personally responsible for our _____

_____

Do you think it is too difficult to change our thoughts, feelings and actions? Do you think it is a constraint if we are not capable of doing this? When an event occur, will you STOP, then change the _____ change the _____ change the _____.

What keeps you from taking the steps to change?

_____

_____

As you start piecing together the missing link, think about what it will take to see transformation truly occur. Write out some behavior changes necessary for transformation. If you put a covenant into place, what change will need to take place for the covenant process to be successful no matter with whom you are dealing, *especially* if they have no clue of the covenant process.

_____

_____

_____

_____

CHAPTER THIRTEEN: *How We Communicate!*

Angela and Linda had a strong interaction. Think back on the last interaction you've had with someone and what your body language, tone of voice and words were actually saying. According to research, we communicate through our body language, tone of voice and actual words. What percentage of the message is being communicated through body language, tone of voice and actual words?

Body Language_____%

Tone of voice_____%

Actual words_____%

Think about the times you have had an argument with a loved one. Could you tell that person was mad at you even if they did not say a word? Why? What did their **body language** convey?

_____

_____

Now think about email, our favorite form of communication. What is the percentage of the message being communicated in **words** alone?_____ What implication does that have with email?

_____

_____

What about talking on the phone? Can you hear when someone is smiling or is angry when they are on the phone? What percentage was **tone** of voice?

Now combine all three and think about how we communicate. If we truly believe our message is important, how we deliver it will make all the difference in the world.

What are some behavior changes you may need to make in order for your messages to be clearly conveyed?

CHAPTER FOURTEEN: *Digging Deeper on Subtle Truths First Impressions*

A first impression is sometimes referred to as a "moment of truth" because people believe that what they are hearing, seeing, or feeling is reality – that is, the truth of the situation. It doesn't matter that their first impression is merely a snapshot of less than one moment in time. It is perceived as genuine: who we are, the quality of service that we deliver or our environment of care. Making that first impression a good one is crucial.

How long does it take to form a first impression? _____

How many additional encounters do you think it takes to undo a negative first impression?

_____

Think of a specific time when someone made a very poor first impression with you. What did you think?? How did you feel about that person? How did that negative impression affect your relationship with that individual?

What is the tool the team discussed to shorten the number of times it takes for us to undo a bad first impression?

_____

What is the tie-in between social anxiety, the hippocampus, first impressions, and the change theory?

CHAPTER FIFTEEN: *Personal Growth Your challenge:* WHAT ARE YOU WILLING TO DO THAT NO ONE ELSE IS WILLING TO DO THAT CAN SET YOU APART?

This is the fun part, the journey inside. The team took a look at what caused them to be anxious, how they wanted to treat each other, how they handled conflict, what happened when an event occurred that was packed with emotion and remained in the long term memory, how important first impressions are, and how we communicate. So what's next?
The team went a bit deeper in order to understand personal growth.

The first step is looking inside which is always more difficult than looking outside. It is tough to acknowledge that a constraint exists.

This first step is _____ :or... **See it or Get a clue!**

The second step is to accept responsibility and exercise control.

The second step is _____ :or... **Own it or Get a grip!**

The third step is to make a commitment to action!

The third step is _____ :or... **Change it or Get a life!**

Sometimes it may be our kids, our spouse, friends, God...whoever is honest and loves us enough to tell us we've got lettuce in our teeth.

When you are willing to take these three steps will you accept what you "see" and change what needs to be changed?_____

How do you plan to do that?

_____

_____

CHAPTER SIXTEEN: *Acknowledging Anger and Fear*

Can you remember the stories everyone shared around the fire pit? Could you relate to any of the memories they shared?

_____

_____

Why do memories and their subsequent emotions burrow so deep within us? Did any of the stories stir up memories for you? Share your thoughts with your group or bumper person

_____

_____

Why was Stuart so afraid? What caused him to be fearful of the dark?

_____

What are the three things that cause anger?

_____

If you know that anger is caused by these three things, what will you do next time you are confronted by someone who is angry?

_____

When you feel yourself getting angry, what are the steps you can take to alleviate your fear, frustration, or pain?

_____

Can you see how hidden anger can fester in a team or a family? What can you do about that?

_____

CHAPTER SEVENTEEN: *A Glorious Morning!*

Did the team seem more comfortable with affirmations? Why?

_____

Why do we get so frustrated with others when we are not responsible for what other people do?

_____

_____

What is it about how we process what others are saying or doing to us that causes us to get frustrated or upset?

_____

CHAPTER EIGHTEEN: *Self-Identity*

What is self identity and how is it formed:

1. _____: The thoughts I believe to be true about myself as a result of

_____

2._____: The thoughts I think about myself as

_____

3. _____: The thoughts I believe to be true about myself based on

_____

How often do you think your self-identity is impacted?

_____

Make a list of 5-10 positive self-concepts about yourself and 10 negative self-concepts. Now share and discuss the list with your bumper person, spouse or a close friend or relative.

Did you have many more negative attributes than positive or vice versa?

Many times you will find your greatest liability is also your greatest asset. Why is that?

How do you suggest we "fix" a potential liability in order to keep it an asset?

What happens when someone gives you feedback? What happens if you don't agree with them? Do we all hear feedback equally? How do we discern how and what we hear?

REMEMBER: Change is a _____, not an _____. More along the lines of a metamorphosis, similar to a butterfly. It takes time.

The only way our self-identity can change is if we surround ourselves with people who are truthful, what we call bumper people. Are you willing to get into relationships with people who are willing to bring you the truth? How would you like to have a positive self-identity?

CHAPTER NINETEEN: *Leadership*

The team had a great discussion about the definition of leadership. What is the definition of leadership?

_____

Think through the leaders that you know and admire. Do you believe they are examples of the definition above? Why or why not?

_____

CHAPTER TWENTY: *V-STTEELE and Lead*

We'd like to help you think way beyond the bubble about leadership. List the various steps (we helped you with the first step):

Cast vision (WHY)...then

S—
T—   **WHAT**
T—   **HOW**
E—   **WHEN, WHERE, WHO**
E—
L—   **Ties it altogether: WHY,**
E—   **WHAT, HOW, WHEN,**
                          WHERE, & WHO

Explain the various steps of leadership and how they equate to WHY, WHAT, HOW, WHEN, WHERE AND WHO.

As a leader, it is important to give people the tools they need and then get out of the way. Make sure you check back and evaluate their progress, see how they're doing.

How can you change your leadership behavior to better serve those around you?

_____

_____

_____

Empowerment has a cost. It entails having a clear understanding of who has taken responsibility for doing what.

How can we move from delegation to empowerment to holding people accountable?

_____

Are you at a place with your leadership that you feel comfortable surrounding yourself with people who may be smarter, more effective than you are?

_____

Walking this out will mean changing our perspective and all that we may have learned about leadership previously.

Let's see how this plays out in our organizations: Draw the three models Joshua shared with the team:

In these models, where is the leader?

Where is the client?

What is the leader doing?

What is happening throughout the organization?

According to the purpose of leadership, what is the leader doing in each of the models?

In which model(s) does the leader cast vision, serve, teach, train, equip, empower, leave, evaluate?

Empower is allowing those you serve to use the tools.

What is the most important part of these organizational models? (HINT: The lines between bubbles represent _____...strong, healthy, whole _____).

Which comes first? Form or function? _____

Function means the particular purpose for which a person or thing is specially fitted or used or for which a thing exists

Form(ation) means an arrangement of persons or things in a prescribed manner or for a certain purpose

Decide function THEN form.

Decide what functions you need in order to run your company and then decide how and who can be in that function.

Why can't you move from the first organizational model directly to the "bubble" chart?

_____

So what keeps us from setting up a healthy functional environment?

_____

_____

CHAPTER TWENTY ONE: *Laying Down Your Life*

What transformation took place for Doug and why?

_____

_____

Do you believe Stuart really wanted to kill himself? What kept him from letting go on the cliff and ending it all?

_____

_____

What happened to Linda and Stuart during the incident on the mountain?

_____

_____

Have you ever been to Neverland, that place where you said things like, "I'll *never* steal, I'll *never* get drunk...or I'll *never* have an affair?

What things have you said you would never do that you ended up doing?

_____

_____

What happened that knocked you off track?

_____

_____

Did you keep it to yourself? If so, why? And what happened due to not sharing?

_____

_____

What keeps us from sharing things hidden so deep within us?

_____

_____

The distance between _____ self and _____ self is directly related to the amount of _____ in our lives.

Do you have an image of your ideal self but are living at a lower level of your real self and feeling stress and anxiety? Why?

_____

What happens to our bodies (our gas tanks) when we experience stress?

S _____

A _____

A_____

D_____

S_____

What are the ways we can keep our gas tank full?

_____

_____

List out what empties your gas tank. Commit to keeping your gas tank full and being a filler to others!

_____

_____

_____

What are Bumper People and why do we need them?

_____

Bumper people will "bump" you back on the right path. Bumper people are people who love you, and who share the truth. They share the "lettuce in your teeth" moment. It's up to you how close you keep those bumper people.

How is this different than accountability?

_____

Why do we keep our bumper people at arm's length (or beyond)?

_____

We think it is safe to keep people at a distance. We may have been hurt in the past and we don't trust people or we're embarrassed or it is just plain P_____

_____

Why is it that we struggle with being close and transparent with others? Now be specific to your life. Why are people kept at a distance in your life?

_____

_____

Stuart struggled with several issues. List them and discuss why they caused him fear, anger, doubt, lust and pride.

_____

_____

_____

CHAPTER TWENTY TWO: *Freedom in Forgiveness!*

Go back to where you identified the constraints of each character. Did you see transformation take place in each of their lives? List each character and what took place and why:

_____

_____

_____

_____

Similar to what each character did, list out one to three things you will change and ask you bumper person to help you.

_____

_____

_____

CHAPTER TWENTY THREE: *Launching!*

What excuse did Stuart give for having an affair?

_____

_____

_____

Why do you think Stuart was hesitant to have Abe call to see if he had talked to his wife about his affair?

_____

What advice did Abe give Stuart?

_____

_____

Did Stuart follow through on what he said he needed to change?

_____

_____

Was he transformed?

_____

Do you believe you can experience transformation? Why or why not?

_____

_____

What is holding you back from experiencing this transformation?

_____

_____

If you've agreed you can experience this transformation, what are your next steps to walking out this process and who are your bumper people to help you see this through?

_____

_____

What is the Missing Link?

_____

_____

_____

33313750R00127

Made in the USA
Charleston, SC
11 September 2014